THE CLUB VAN CORTLANDT

John Borek

The Club Van Cortlandt

First Edition Paperback 978-1-935355-36-6

Ebook 978-1-935355-30-4

New Shelves Books
Rochester, NY 14610

The author has tried to recreate events, locales and conversations from memories of them. In order to maintain their anonymity in some instances the author has changed the names of individuals and places. The author may have also changed some identifying characteristics and details such as physical properties, occupations and places of residence.

Cover art design by Louie Podlaski

Manufactured and Printed in the United States of America.
Library of Congress Control Number and PCIP on file with publisher

"To make his magic, fiction, look real the artist sometimes places it, as Tolstoy does within a definite historical frame, citing facts that can be checked in a library—that citadel of illusion."

–Vladimir Nabokov,
Lectures on Russian Literature

To Jackie

Who

Let Me Live

John Borek

Chapter One

That summer, after our first college year, Bertrand, Joan and I decided to pull a *Jules and Jim*, albeit one without sex, murder or suicide.

Movies were the cultural language of our youth, so it was less than a coincidence that we had each independently seen Truffaut's ode to free love that spring. We thought the living arrangement would suit us once we modified it for middle-class American teenage scruples.

We moved out of our homes and into Bertrand's fallen-upon-hard-times cottage on the shores of Silver Lake. The cottage had been suspended in amber right after the '29 crash and had just barely been kept in Bertrand's family. It was populated with artifacts of past wealth, like leather-bound complete editions of Dickens and Lord Macaulay's *History of England* along with an enormous collection of Tin Pan Alley sheet music that complemented the volumes of *Godey's Lady's Books* and Gibson Girl portfolios that lay untouched for decades on the bookshelves. Until now.

I spent the summer reading through the Dickens. Bertrand spent the summer smoking and making the sheet music come to life through the warped upright piano. Joan spent the summer working the lunch counter at an early version of a discount department store to keep us in funds. Jules and Jim never had it so good.

Bertrand's large, happy, frayed family would come every weekend to drink and to watch the silver water, occasionally take a modest boat out on it, or roller skate at the pre-Great War skating rink. None of them seemed to censor or care about our living arrangements. But, then, the family subscribed to *The New Yorker*.

When it came time to say goodbye, our trinity did not cry. Of course, we didn't know we would never have a summer like this again.

Before I left school that spring, I had signed a lease for an apartment on 113th Street. Do I have to say, sight unseen? But my soon-to-be mates, Grant and Wu, assured me it was the deal of the century. My parents were unhappy with my decision to leave Carman Hall and the safety of security guards, but I was determined to live the life of a real New Yorker. At nineteen, I was a leaseholder.

Unlike freshman year, I had no parents accompany me. Bill drove me from Rochester to 113th Street in one of his series of decrepit Peugeots which were always missing essentials like tailpipes, windshield wipers or brakes. Bill had nothing better to do since he had dropped out of Bard and was busy losing fifty pounds to avoid the draft. He did succeed in looking skeletal helped by emetics and LSD. We stopped every hour on the way down so he could induce vomiting.

I was the first to arrive at the apartment. Grant and Wu told me we were subletting from a very, very, very short Filipino. They were right. I rang the buzzer for 4G. The very, very, very short Filipino met me on the stoop. I gave him $300 as Grant and Wu had done earlier in the summer, and he gave me the key. I thought it odd that after the key exchange, he bade me goodbye and didn't go up to the apartment to show me the various quirks that come with any new residence. He said "Enjoy" and gave a laugh as little as he was. Then he disappeared.

I took the elevator to the fourth floor, walked down the cheap green paint hallways and found the dark-red peeling wooden door of 4G. I put the key in the lock, opened the door and felt the thrill of impending adulthood and freedom.

For all of thirty seconds.

Chapter Two

The Sexual Freedom League was founded in the early 1960s in New York and then, like all things extreme, migrated to Berkeley a few years later. Eventually, the League bifurcated. One branch, the Berkeley branch, was political and fought for contraceptive and abortion rights, homosexual rights and free love, unbinding adultery from traditional marriage into an open marriage or no marriage at all. It saw itself in an honest tradition established by, among others, the Oneida Community and Bertrand Russell. The other branch, the New York branch, whose members included Allen Ginsberg and the Living Theater guru, Julian Beck, only believed in orgies.

I knew none of this when I opened the door to 4G. Like many New York apartments, most rooms were connected by a very long hall. I sensed this hall in front of me when I fumbled for the light switch and turned on the lights. I was disoriented for a moment because the light was dim, but I gradually made out that the hallway was covered in burlap and pinned to the burlap were hundreds of cream-colored opaque water balloons that all seemed to have liquid in them.

This was the first time I would see a spent condom. And the only time I would see hundreds filled with sperm. Yes. Grant and Wu had rented the New York headquarters of the Sexual Freedom League, Orgy Division.

I turned on the lights in room after room of the large apartment only to find stained sheetless mattresses and bundles of pornography. I went into the kitchen and opened the refrigerator door and hundreds of insects poured out. I doubt that Stephen King, Dean Koontz and Clive Barker working together could imagine such a horror.

I sat on an empty box that crumbled beneath my weight. I started to cry. Classes started tomorrow and my parents were visiting in five days.

Bill returned from parking the Peugeot. "Yuk," he said when he walked into the apartment. "This is disgusting." He bent down and picked up a small piece of paper. It was a membership card for The Sexual Freedom League of New York with a member's name and an official signature of the Secretary of the organization.

"I can't stay. This is disgusting," he repeated. We unloaded my suitcases, my typewriter and seven boxes of books. I was soon alone.

There was very little to do but to start cleaning. I went to the firehouse next door to ask where a hardware store was. I was directed to Amsterdam Avenue. I bought a mop, garbage bags, sponges, cleaning liquid. It took me two trips to bring the supplies back.

I started by unpinning the used condoms from the burlap. At this point, Grant and Wu arrived. After a cursory tour of the disaster area, Grant announced they would find find somewhere else to stay. They didn't even make copies of the key. I knew they would never be back.

I had five days. I went into overdrive. I managed to attend classes but cleaned instead of doing my assigned reading. Whenever I got depressed, I'd crack open a Modern Library Giant of six plays by George S. Kaufman and Moss Hart. In this way I made it through *The Man Who Came to Dinner*, *You Can't Take It With You*, and *George Washington Slept Here*, laughing through my tears. Or crying through my laughter.

By the time my parents got there on Saturday morning, the apartment looked pretty good. Walls were cracked, paint was peeling, but you'd never know a thousand sex acts had taken place within these rooms. Even the burlap looked sort of trendy. The refrigerator had been the biggest challenge. I removed countless cockroaches from its interior and its motor with a pair of tweezers. Who knew cockroaches liked compressors as much as food?

Grant and Wu informed me they had found a new place to live—a fraternity on 114th Street. There had been only two places open but they had talked to the leadership and the fraternity would probably accept me as their next pledge. But they anticipated no available rooms until next year.

There was no furniture in the apartment which had the odd effect of making it seem modern and airy. I had dragged out the stained mattresses, broken chairs and corduroy floor pillows. I had stocked the pantry, thumbtacked a few posters to the walls, and put my books in milk crates. I hung my few clothes in a closet and borrowed a sleeping bag for my bedroom. The bathroom had toilet paper the kitchen, paper towels.

My mother still cried. And cried and cried and cried. After a tour of the neighborhood and a quick lunch at Tom's Diner, they returned to their protective exoskeleton, the New York Hilton at Avenue of the Americas and 53rd.

My parents left around 3 p.m. that afternoon. I was reading, or rather trying to read, a very abridged version of *Principles of Mathematics* for my Chemistry for Poets' class. I reflected on how Russell's sexual principles got me into this mess in the first place.

There was a knock on the door.

I got up and tome in hand, opened it. There was a man out of Dashiell Hammett. Sam Spade stood in front of me.

"Is Magtanggol de la Rosa here, also known as Matt Rose?"

"No," I replied, adding that I'd never heard of such a person.

"Are you sure? He's four feet tall and from the Philippines," he added.

Thinking that no good would come of admitting I was renting the apartment from him, I remained silent.

"Do you know where he is?"

"No," I quite truthfully replied.

"Then I am serving you with his eviction notice from this apartment."

He handed me a legal document in a blue paper binder, turned around and walked down the stairs.

I stood in the doorway thinking about The Heisenberg Uncertainty Principle and then blacked out.

When I recovered, I went downstairs and walked to the corner of Amsterdam Avenue where there was a phone booth. I called the New York Hilton and asked for Mr. Borek's room. When my father answered, I told him I had just been evicted. I heard him yell to my mother "Johnny's been thrown out of his apartment." I heard my mother whisper, "Thank you, Lord."

My father told me to pack up everything immediately and take a cab to the Hilton and call their room when I arrived. I had not thrown out any of my boxes, so it was easy and quick to re-pack seven boxes of books. I threw my clothes and personal items back into the two suitcases and rolled up my sleeping bag after vigorously shaking it out.

My typewriter, an IBM Selectric Business model with "unique typeball technology," was a challenge. My father had bought it used from his workplace for fifty dollars. It was not portable or rather portable only for weightlifters. Bill had helped me bring it upstairs. I kicked it to the elevator, then kicked it to the stoop. I hailed a cab, asked the cabbie to help me lift the IBM into the trunk, loaded books and suitcases and sleeping bag into the back seat and squeezed myself into the front seat.

I had now joined the armies of New Yorkers who have relocated by taxi.

I never did read the three remaining Kaufman and Hart plays.

By the time the taxi pulled up in the Hilton's portico, I was a basket case. My heart was racing and I was hyperventilating. I told the bellman I needed to take my cabful of belongings to Mr. Borek's room. When he opened the trunk and saw the monstrous one-eyed IBM Selectric, he called two younger men over to lift it. And so, boxes of books, typewriter, suitcases and sleeping bag went on the luggage cart. I looked like a youthful literary refugee. And I was.

My parents had a small suite. They called maid service and had the sofa in the parlor made up for me. My parents had a business dinner planned so they told me not to leave and to order room service. They came back late. I barely noticed.

I stayed in the parlor the whole of Sunday and then when Monday morning came, I announced that I was dropping out.

"We'll find a place for you to live," my father said. "Whatever it takes." They left to make good on their promise.

They canvassed blocks of the Upper West Side on foot. They read the want ads; they rang supers' bells; they went to campus housing forlornly begging for a dorm room. These are all things I should have done, but being a crown prince for so long had left me without survival skills.

At just about five p.m., they came back and announced that they had found a place and I could move in immediately. The bellman came up to the room and we loaded everything we had unloaded into a new cab.

My parents gave me a business card with my new home's address and a twenty, bade me farewell and I made my way to 549 West 113th Street.

I was now a resident of the Club Van Cortlandt.

Chapter Three

The Club Van Cortlandt was built in 1908 as a residential hotel by the architect Benjamin Levitan, who also built the Women's House of Detention at Greenwich and West 10th where at various times the executed "spy" Ethel Rosenberg, the Black activist Angela Davis and Andy Warhol's assailant Valerie Solanas were all confined. The Club Van Cortlandt was one step above that prison on the architectural food chain.

There were seven floors, six residential. The building was constructed around a courtyard, presumably to make the structure light and airy, but the windows were so filthy that the general effect was that of living in a coal mine in winter and on an oil slick in warm weather.

Each floor had three deluxe suites which consisted of one large room, a large-ish bathroom, and a kitchenette with a tenement sink, an ancient refrigerator and a leaky stove. On either side of these suites were parallel corridors which each revealed six single rooms, a common bathroom and a common kitchen. Because of their shared amenities, these rooms were much cheaper. And because of their price, they were in high demand by desperate souls. I had a suite so I was on the low end of desperation and, consequently, greatly envied.

I emptied out my belongings on the curb, ran in and got a hand truck from the super. But before I could take possession of 3B, I had to contend with the concierge. Concierge is probably too snooty a word for Dorothy Dutto, who was generally called The Lady in the Cage. She spent her daylight hours in a three square-foot freestanding booth with a very thick metal grille where she faced her audience. There was just enough space under the grille to slide a rent check or, perhaps, a bribe. With no disrespect to Ethel Merman, she looked like Ms. Merman on a bad day. Uncombed bright red hair, a housedress, a Brooklynese voice that would melt metal. And as I was soon to discover because she showed me, an illegal switchblade tucked into the top of her pantyhose. She had five sons and they were all policemen. I'll leave it to you to guess if they were good cops or bad cops.

"Your parents are so nice. Your mother is such a lady. I AIN'T GONNA HAVE ANY TROUBLE WITH YOU, AM I? YOU'RE NOT A COMMUNIST HIPPIE, ARE YOU?"

"No, ma'am, I'm a student" and with that she gave me the key.

I opened the door to my second apartment that month with increased trepidation. The hallway was narrow, with a tin fleur-de-lis wallcovering painted in mental hospital green. Unsurprisingly, 3B was between 3A and 3C. There were open corridors on either side that, for now, would be left unexplored.

I went in and turned on the light. I have since seen rooms similar to this in British films of the 1930s. This was like a super deluxe bed-sitting room if by deluxe you meant merely depressing instead of suicidal. Although it was not quite dark outside, it was quite dark inside.

There were two single beds—metal frame beds with flophouse mattresses. The beds were diametrically opposed to make sure there was no mistaking intimacy. One bed was nearest the door; one was farthest from the door near the window. There was a threadbare factory-made Oriental rug that looked like it was taken from my grandparents' living room. A metal kitchen table was shoved up against the windows and graced with two wobbly kitchen chairs. The room itself had recently been painted mental hospital brown, a nice enhancement to the hallway. There were the windows themselves—one large flanked by two small window panels all of which looked as if they had been cleaned by rags soaked in 40 weight motor oil and then breaded with dirt. There was a fire escape landing right outside these windows. There were no window locks.

The cooking area consisted of a kitchen alcove with a stove and an exposed plumbing sink. Alow alcove wall had some shelves facing out into the room and some shelves near the stove that were covered in sticky-backed decorative paper adorned with cheerless flowers. There was a gasping refrigerator from the era just after iceboxes.

And then there was the bathroom. Sparkling white, dense with white tiles, a huge bathtub and a presentable toilet. I could always live in the bathroom, I thought.

After I negotiated Mrs. Dutto and after I put my 35 pound Selectric on the kitchen table and breathed a sigh of relief when the table didn't buckle, I left. I walked down to 110th Street, to the street-level apartment of my freshman roommate Nathaniel, who had signed a lease with my Catholic freshman collabo, Connor. Theirs was a gorgeous New York apartment with inlaid hardwood floors, spacious rooms and an upgraded modern kitchen. They had taken on a third Columbia student Peter, who at 5'2" held down the *On the Waterfront* roommate position with his slicked back hair, wire-rimmed glasses, and a motorcycle much larger than he was which he parked in the step-down living room.

Nathaniel and Connor had told me the year before that they were not going to ask me to room with them because they thought I was too intense. I wasn't really offended because shortly afterward Grant and Wu asked me to apartment pool.

But now I felt like crap. Nathaniel asked to take a walk with me. We walked up Riverside Drive and he told me the story of his losing his virginity the week before. It had something to do with *The Fantasticks*, a show he had stayed in New York to understudy that summer and a woman a decade older named Joanne who was the estranged wife of one of the producers. Nathaniel was not particularly virile, so when he concluded "I think I'm in love" I thought it sounded like the beginning of another song from *The Fantasticks*.

Now I was depressed beyond diagnosis: no cool New York apartment, no ten-year-older girlfriend, no motorcycle. Just me, a shabby room and my IBM Selectric.

When I got back to The Club, the door to my apartment was ajar. In fact, the lock had been jimmied and the door frame was cracked. When I went inside, I saw that the window on the fire escape was open. My boxes of books were overturned; the contents of my suitcases were scattered around the room.

There was an empty space on the kitchen table. It took me a moment to realize that my thirty-five pound IBM Selectric was gone. Someone had actually spirited it down the fire escape. I wondered for a moment if the thief was a literary type or rather, typist. Maybe my thief was a budding Villon or Genet, or maybe even a Dostoyevsky.

I turned around and noticed a mimeoed piece of paper on the floor by the door. I picked it up. It read:

> *The Club Van Cortlandt is DANGEROUS. We have experienced a string of burglaries in the last month that have victimized many tenants in the building. We live in fear. Join us tonight at 7 pm in Room 304A to discuss ways we can make the owners provide us with protection. Signed, Andrew Hosey, President, Club Van Cortlandt Tenants' Association.*

My room had been broken into while the tenants were being distracted by a tenants' association meeting. I immediately suspected Mr. Hosey of arranging a last-minute meeting with an accomplice who then hit the jackpot in my room and spirited my IBM Selectric down three flights of death-defying iron-retractable fire stairs. I put the notice on my barren kitchen table, shoved my boxes of books against the broken door and climbed onto one of the beds and went to sleep without pulling back the faded chenille bedspread. It had been a long, long day.

The next morning, I dutifully reported the burglary to Mrs. Dutto who, despite having five sons, any one of whom could have written a police report, did not call the police. "Twenty-five to fix the door and fifty more if you want a police lock." A police lock I discovered was a metal bar about three-and-a-half feet long. It was installed at a sixty degree angle between the floor and the door. It was a primitive barricade and unassailable. Too late, but unassailable.

As for the fire escape windows, she told me to go to the hardware store and ask for some "sticks." I did. The sticks were simple dowels they pre-cut for Van Cortlandt tenants. "How d'ya like The Club, kid?" and before I could answer I saw a wink passed around the employees.

The dowels went diagonally in the window frames. The windows would be made secure and I could just pop one out if the place caught fire. A fire began to seem likely to me.

I returned to The Club with my dowels. Mrs. Dutto was arguing with an unkempt man about forty. The man was screaming something about the tenants' association. "We're going to sue; we're going to win and we're going to fire you."

Mrs. Dutto kindly replied, "We never should have rented to a PERVERT like you. You PERVERT. We'll get you on a morals. I'll have my sons see to it."

"Fuck you, Mrs. Dutto," the unkempt man said from the safety of the elevator. It stopped at the third floor, my floor.

That was Andrew Hosey, President, Club Van Cortlandt Tenants' Association. He became, for the next three years, my best, sometimes my only friend.

Chapter Four

It is difficult to describe unattractive people. It violates a basic moral tenet. People can't help what they look like. Andy was unattractive. He looked like any character actor who played the town drunk, even though I never once saw him drink. He had a permanent five-day stubble, beady eyes and the skin tone of Huckleberry Finn's Pap—that is, fish-belly white. Andy was not tall; he was not short. His considerable belly overhung his belt and he wore unpressed chinos. He most always wore a cheap short-sleeved shirt over a short-sleeved undershirt. Oh, and he had a postnasal drip that evidenced itself twice a sentence. Andy was a mess.

"Have anything to do with him and I'll call your parents," Dutto yelled after me as I took the stairs.

When I opened the door to my room, there was a woman in my bed. At least I thought it was a woman. When I leaned over to wake her, I smelled whiskey.

She turned toward me, and I realized she must be about 80. She was Black and wearing an Aunt Jemima head schmatta. She looked like a Black Mammy Yokum from the dyspeptic L'il Abner comics.

"Who are you?"

She answered, "Clarabelle."

"What are you doing here?"

"Miss Dutto told me to clean your room."

"Miss" was pronounced with three syllables.

I then noticed an old-fashioned push/pull carpet sweeper.

"Let me get you some water."

"I'm FINE," she yelled at me. "Just restin'. Don't tell Miss Dutto."

I had no reason to tell Miss Dutto anything because she would just tell my parents.

"I won't," I promised.

There was a sign in the entrance to the lobby advertising The Club Van Cortlandt. If you looked very carefully, under its name it said in tiny italics *Complete Hotel Services*.

Clarabelle was the living, breathing, walking embodiment of how complete the hotel services were.

Andy's curriculum vitae from the fragments he scattered:

> Andy was born in California's Central Valley near Stockton. By four, he was discovered to be a double prodigy in mathematics and music. By sixteen, he had graduated from the California University system with a Master's in Mathematics and moved to Italy where he studied at the Music Conservatory of Perugia and quickly was elevated to a teaching position. He travelled extensively giving piano concerts throughout Europe. He made several recordings. Some time in his mid-twenties, he began having symptoms of schizophrenia. By his late twenties, he had left Italy and had moved to New York to explore the work of psychoanalyst Wilhelm Reich. He thought Reich could resolve or control his schizophrenia.

He lived on welfare which at the time was quite generous. Andy was able to eat in restaurants, and most importantly to him, have new underwear every day. I don't know how long he had been living in The Club when I got there, but he became a very big thorn in the owners' sides. He organized a tenants' association and filed a lawsuit. The lawsuit made him an untouchable in a good way and a bad way. It would be difficult to evict him from his small room. But he also never got Clarabelle's cleaning services.

The arc of Andy's life was made word when a week or so after I met him, he knocked on my door. He was very nervous.

"I wonder if you'd help me," he asked.

"Sure," I said. I asked him to come in and offered him a Coke.

"I'm invited to this function and I need a tuxedo. There's a men's store down the street that rents tuxes but a year or so ago I, uh, had a dispute with them. I thought if you went with me and we each got a tuxedo I could sort of squeak through."

"I don't need a tuxedo," I answered rather obviously.

"You can come to the function too. I can bring a guest." He handed me the invitation. It read in part:

> **Come Celebrate the Greatest Pianist in the World, Vladimir Horowitz, before his first televised concert ever at Carnegie Hall.**

I paused. "Sure."

We went to the men's store and, as Andy had predicted, when I went in first and spoke for us, the owner was reluctant to make a scene. And our money was good. We got the cheapest tuxedos in the shop.

When the evening came, we decided to walk. The invitation was for 5 p.m. and the Horowitz house was in the Nineties on the Upper East Side. I recognized the address from a biography I had been reading of George S. Kaufman after I had lost interest in reading his plays. Before Horowitz, Kaufman lived there.

Normally I would have had reservations about walking down 110th Street along the north end of Central Park wearing a tuxedo. But we left the Club at four in the afternoon and there were two of us. When we got to the address, it was an impressive, though narrow, white stone townhouse. I had never been in a townhouse before.

Before I could knock or ring, the door was opened smoothly by a liveried manservant. He asked for our invitation. Andy spent a panicked thirty seconds looking for it, but finally produced it. The manservant welcomed us skeptically.

Not ten feet in front of us was Mr. Horowitz. He looked up at his new guests, stared right past me and then saw Andy. His face lit up.

"ANDEEEEE!" he shouted. And then he just walked away from whomever he was talking to and came over to hug and kiss my charge. "Andee, I miss you SO MUCH!" he said with that Russian burr in his throat.

Andy introduced me, but Vladimir took no notice. He spirited Andy away to see his wife Wanda who was equally thrilled. I saw them all retreat to the back of the room. I was left to my own devices. Nineteen, with long unkempt hair, wearing a rented tuxedo and standing among the most important cultural figures in New York. And I didn't recognize a one.

I wandered around for a while. Three people asked me to get them drinks, which I did. I followed around the help trying to eat two each of the many different hors d'oeuvres. I looked at the painting above the mantel. I thought "that looks like a real Picasso." It was. I asked for a Coke.

Finally, Andy emerged from the crowd. "Ready to go," he declared. "That was great seeing Volodya. It's been years."

We took a cab back to the Club. Neither of us had a television so we watched the live broadcast in the room of my newest Van Cortlandt friend, Pat. We barely found a place to sit among her sculptures. The broadcast was on CBS. Half of America was watching.

I still remember that Horowitz played Chopin that night.

Chapter Five

Around this time, I had a girlfriend. Yes, reader, I know you are surprised, but give me a break, even Kafka had a girlfriend.

Her name was Evelyn, Evie for short. I met her on the first day of a class I was taking at Barnard. The New Testament. I was not particularly interested in Jesus, but I was interested in meeting young women.

The professor, who was herself a young woman, asked us to pair off for an exercise in which we listed what we already knew about the New Testament. This type of exercise usually precedes explosive revelations about a topic that leaves you reeling. Joseph was a mason, not a carpenter. Mary wore red, not blue. Gabriel was announced by a saxophone, not a trumpet.

I paired off with Evie. We had an entertaining ten minutes in which we bantered about humility and crucifixion. We lingered after class and walked out together.

We all have requirements for the person we hope will complete us. Evie resembled my wonderful high school girl friends—non-romantic category—with an additional spark of physical attraction.

The requirements Evie fulfilled were:

1. She laughed at my jokes.
2. She was funny on her own.
3. She liked to talk.
4. She wasn't flirtatious.
5. She had a low voice.
6. She was smart.
7. She was Jewish.

(I will now take a narrative break to say these qualities were condensed, refined and super-concentrated in Jacqueline Levine, my spouse of 42 years as of this writing, in the year of our Lord, 2018.)

We found ourselves walking down Broadway toward her apartment. When we got to the building's door, a young Black man emerged. He was pretty Black Power looking. Jeans, a dashiki, an awesome Afro. He saw Evie, walked over to her, kissed her and said, "Later, babe. I made you lunch."

In my mind, I drew a thin line through the word "relationship."

The topic of our next class was soteriology, or the study of salvation. I was pleasant to Evie but a little distant. I tried to concentrate on the ways one could be saved.

At the end of class, she walked up to me and said, "I don't want you to get the wrong idea. Pontius and I are just friends."

"Pontius? Like Pontius Pilate?"

"No, like Pontius Jacobs. You know, the friend in front of my building."

"Oh," I said trying to sound nonchalant.

"I mean, we live together and sleep in the same bed, but we're not boyfriend and girlfriend. We're just good friends."

Long before the invention of the acronym TMI, I thought, "Too much information."

Unbelievable? Perhaps. But, my child, it was the late Sixties. It made perfect sense, in an imperfect way. They both got hipster status from their respective communities and from the college community in general. Evie, I later learned, was running for Class Vice-President. This would give her a nice political hook.

I was still silent. I needed to be pursued.

"Would you like to go to an oboe concert?" she asked.

"Sure," I replied.

Salvation.

You have no idea how many oboe concerts there are on any given night in Manhattan. On both the Barnard and

Columbia campuses. At the Manhattan School of Music near campus, the Donnell Library by the Museum of Modern Art, the sculpture garden of the Museum of Modern Art, Town Hall, Carnegie Hall, any church that needs a few extra bucks. And the combos. Oboe and piano, oboe and continuo, oboe and orchestra, two oboes, two oboes with two English horns, two clarinets, two bassoons; woodwind quartets. Even Scott Joplin's *The Entertainer* had an oboe. Who knew?

The girl sure liked oboes.

A lot of this was foreplay. We could not go to Evie's apartment because Pontius was there sleeping in her bed and even though I had my room, Mrs. Dutto reigned. She often stayed in her cage until 9 p.m. and though it was none of her business, if we went upstairs on her watch, she would yell out, "NO ORGIES." Only she pronounced or-ghee as if you took the P off of Porgy of "Porgy and Bess."

One night Evie did stay over. She decided this would be The Night. Only she quite rightly insisted that I have protection. I was not the kind of young man who confidently carried condoms in his wallet, so I excused myself and said I would secure said protection.

It was after 9 p.m. New York may be the City That Never Sleeps, but then in the late Sixties it was The City You Couldn't Buy a Fucking Condom In After 9 p.m. Please remember there were no cell phones and no data banks to conjure up 24-hour pharmacies. I ran around like a sex-crazed rooster looking for open drugstores only to find myself farther and farther down Broadway. There was also no way to call Evie. After 45 minutes, I put my movie-going experience to good use and took the IRT to Times Square. Here even the pretzel vendors sold condoms. This was condom Nirvana. I chose some plain janes from a newsstand and waited an eternity on the subway platform to go back uptown.

By the time I returned, it was after eleven. Evie was sound asleep. I mean sound asleep. I went to the single bed on the other side of the room. I fell asleep fully clothed.

When we woke up, it was morning and we realized we had to navigate past Mrs. Dutto. Sure enough when she saw us together, she screamed, "Mr. Borek, I'm going to call your parents and tell them you had an orgy." Once again orgy was bestowed with a hard g.

And she did. She called my parents.

The next time I spoke with my parents, my father took the phone and asked if I had had an orgy. Being unused to the word, he too pronounced it with a hard g. "No," I answered truthfully. "But I do have a girlfriend."

And that was that.

Chapter Six

There comes a time in young man's life when he is invited to meet a young woman's parents. And that time came for me.

Evie's parents invited me for Thanksgiving. The family homestead was in the unfortunately named Long Island hamlet of Hicksville, perhaps a name with even more lack of social cachet than Levittown. Although I'm sure Mr. Hicks was a well-respected member of his community and went to church every Sunday, his legacy undermined the aspirations of a young man who escaped Upstate New York for New York City.

I left Thanksgiving morning on the Long Island Railroad. This was a good decision since the day before the LIRR resembled the flight from India to Pakistan during the Partition.

Evie greeted me at the empty train station and we drove to her family's modest house which resembled my family's modest house. In fact, her featureless street resembled my featureless street.

It was an era when I heard the following short story:

> A young woman's parents came to their daughter's commune for Thanksgiving. Their daughter's boyfriend met them at the door of their yurt stark raving naked. Their daughter did not seem to mind and, in fact, appeared to revel in this gross indecency.

I like to think that she eventually dumped this guy to marry a hedge fund manager. But perhaps she still lives in a yurt. You never know.

I, however, was a perfect gentleman, schooled by Mrs. Botsford's etiquette lessons. But deep inside I wanted to rip my clothes off and run stark raving naked through Hicksville.

The food was good, as it usually is in these situations, since family recipes are involved. The company around the dining room table, that had been supplemented with wobbly card table additions, was a standard assortment of relatives. All was a social blur. Everyone was there for me as much as for the holiday. Part of my novelty was my goyishness. The family was able to prove their progressive credentials by interfaith entertaining.

Evie's older brother punched me in the shoulder a few times and said something about some team that played some sport. He was large. I'm large but he was large in a different way. I tried not to wince and suppressed an urge to ask him if he ever read Tennyson.

Evie's father, an air traffic controller, delivered an odd sort of grace. He welcomed me into the family and announced that Evie had said I was a very nice young man with honorable intentions. Grandmas and grandpas, aunts and uncles, sisters and brothers all nodded. And then for the wind-up, he said "And if his intentions aren't honorable, I've got a rifle in the den."

There was explosive laughter. I looked at the turkey, tried for a nonchalant smile, but saw myself trussed and on the charger. This was the beginning of the end.

After dinner, my novelty wore off. The family dispersed, secure in the knowledge that there had been a suitable match and I briefly exhaled. But before my next inhale, the evening's next act was announced. Evie's mother, previously proudly silent, stepped forward and in a steely gamin way befitting her modish short haircut said, "Why don't you kids go visit the girls. They'd enjoy meeting John."

The girls lived next door. The girls were in their fifties. The girls were busy dismembering the last vestiges of girlhood. The girls were lesbians. And I loved The Girls.

The Girls poured the two of us some scotch, neat, and threw questions at me. And not questions about my upbringing or social status. They were quite interested in the Columbia educational system—two years of common core courses in literature, music, art, philosophy and political science. Adelaide, with grey hair and penetrating green eyes, quizzed me about Rousseau in an attempt to determine if I was more a natural or a civil man. Poppy, who had brown hair and irises as dark as dark chocolate, asked about museums I'd been to. When I was cleaning out the Sexual Freedom League apartment, I had gone for a break to the Museum of Modern Art to see a movie. I was late so I walked through the galleries instead and saw the last day of a show called *The Art of the Real.* This was the first time most people saw Donald Judd, Jasper Johns and Carl Andre in a museum rather than a gallery. Poppy went nuts with questions. She had missed the show.

It turned out that Poppy had trained as a painter at The Arts Student League and when her career went nowhere became an accountant. Adelaide had a Masters in Philosophy. She was now an executive in a clothing firm in the garment district. She said something that I never forgot. It was the best response to how to study the humanities and yet still navigate the world that I've ever heard.

"The day after I walked for my masters, I picked up *The New York Times* and opened it to the want ads. I needed a job. I looked for help wanteds for philosopher-kings. There were none. But there were a lot of entry-level positions for junior executives on Seventh Avenue. I very philosophically chose this path, putting my masters to good use."

I wanted to stay forever in the challenging glow of their lives. Hicksville had a beating heart and a whirring brain. But they lived next door.

I went back to spend the night in the house with a rifle in the den.

After Thanksgiving, I did my best to avoid Evie. I sensed I was one 42nd Street condom away from marriage and fatherhood. And besides, The Girls' urbane, pragmatic and childless lives appealed to me a thousand times more than life around the dinner table at Hicksville. It was not easy to find two weeks of excuses since we still saw each other in class. But collegiate relationships have a way of being put on hold during finals. Also, she was going to Florida for break with her family to see more of her family, so there would be no immediate Hicksville encore and I was not yet a sure enough bet to be invited along on a family vacation.

When I wasn't studying, I threw myself into the social life of the Van Cortlandt, or rather it threw itself at me.

I was in apartment 3B. There were two other rooms with kitchen alcoves and bathrooms on the floor. 3A was occupied by Carmen, a Latina in her mid-thirties who lived there along with her mother. Whenever I walked by and the door was open, I'd see Carmen's mother ironing. Carmen did not look like a firecracker, so it was a surprise to discover that she at least made a part-time living entertaining older Latino men in her room. During these episodes, her mother would bring out a kitchen chair and sit in the hallway. She could not go downstairs because Mrs. Dutto would then know that their visitor was no brother/uncle/

friend of the family. When I came home and mama was in the hallway, we would always exchange polite "holas." Once mama brought over a chicken and rice dish, but that was about it.

3C was inhabited by a man from the Midwest also in his mid-thirties. Dan came to New York to teach seventh grade. And that's all I knew about him. He too was no firecracker . . . with glasses. He never had visitors. He lived in isolation in a way that made me wonder if he had secrets. Did he have to change his identity because of dangerous exploits? Was I living next door to an undercover agent? Was he writing an explosive tell-all book? No, I think Dan was just a dull guy who grabbed a sandwich at Smilers, the corner deli, every evening, and corrected papers all night. His door was never open.

The two corridors in the wings on each end of the third floor were much more fertile hunting grounds. This is where Andy lived and where there were five single rooms even more depressing than mine— 9x12 living spaces each with the standard single bed, one small window, barely large enough for an adult to jump out of and no kitchen or bathroom facilities whatsoever and no hot plates allowed. The five residents shared a kitchen and a bathroom. Cockroaches included.

I hadn't seen Andy for a few days, so I went searching for him. I found him in his room, in bed. He hadn't eaten for a while and his room was filled with quite a few bottles of yellow liquid. Which I quickly realized was urine.

I was emptying the urine and throwing out the bottles when a young man, not more than five or six years older than I was, appeared in the hallway. "Oh, good," he said. "I was coming to do that, but I'm glad you did instead. It made me sick." With that, he came in.

He propped Andy up on his cot, unwrapped a roast beef sandwich and started to tear off small bits and feed him.

"He's clinically depressed," the young man said. And that was my introduction to Tom, who was to be another good friend for more than a decade.

Tom was a graduate student in Clinical Psychology. This made him a perfect compatriot for taking care of Andy. And since Tom was an actual student of depression and anxiety, he had a soothing professional manner that coaxed Andy to eat and use the bathroom.

My eye wandered from the rather intimate feeding tableau to something I had not noticed before. It was a free-standing closet lined in tin with a dining room chair in it.

"What's that?" I asked.

Tom sighed. "That is Andy's Orgone box."

"What's that?" I asked again, realizing that I sounded stupid.

"Well, here goes," Tom patiently answered. He liked long explanations.

"The Orgone box is the invention of a psychoanalyst named Wilhelm Reich. When he was young, he ran Freud's outpatient clinic in Vienna, so he's right up there with Freud and Jung. Unfortunately for him, he started to think about channeling energy from the cosmos in order to cure people. He called the energy orgones and he built these contraptions called Orgone boxes. You sit in a box like that one over there and the cosmic particles are attracted to you. They increase your energy and your libido."

There was a pause

"Sex drive," Tom appended probably fearful that I was going to say "What's that?" again.

Tom continued. "Reich didn't end up well. First, he fled the Nazis for Norway. Then the Norwegians didn't like him, so he fled here and ended up dying in a prison in Pennsylvania for selling these boxes because Americans don't like to think about sex."

I certainly didn't want to think about Andy's sex life, so I nodded in assent.

"Andy says he knew Reich and he built him that box. It's possible."

Andy rallied. "He built that box with his own hands."

Tom continued. "They also carted away six tons of his books here to New York and burned them in an incinerator down in the Village."

"Oh," I said, not wanting to commit myself one way or another.

By this time Andy was recovering. "It's not a contraption," Andy said with irritation. "It can cure cancer. It's a way of communicating with God."

"So you say," Tom said.

I bade them goodnight and walked back to the safe haven of my compressed apartment. As I retreated, they were still arguing.

Chapter Seven

Grant of the Filipino dwarf debacle was trying to make amends for my exile from normal student life. First, he apologized. "The apartment wasn't filled with sex debris when I signed the lease." "It looked like an authentic sublet agreement." "I felt sorry for him because he was so short." So, as reparation, he invited me to his home for Christmas.

I had never spent a Christmas away from home. At first the idea was shocking, compounded by the fact that I owed my parents allegiance since they rescued me from my own threats of dropping out. But then I remembered my father's hands around my throat at the beginning of the summer and our tumble down the cellar stairs and I thought a little distance and a little independence might not be a bad thing. I called them and broke the news with the guilt that only an only child has. They took it well which I gathered to mean they needed a hiatus from me as well. I told them I would be spending most of the break with them but would just miss a few days around Christmas.

I had thought about staying with my Van Cortlandt family for Christmas, but campus would be emptied out and I would have nothing to distract me from loner loneliness. Celebrating with Andy, Tom and Pat in the Van Cortlandt lobby around the Christmas tree that was locked away at 6 p.m. was not a very cheerful vision. And Ms. Dutto was no sugar plum fairy and would surely monitor and misrepresent our celebration to my parents. So I thanked Grant and accepted.

I stopped by Andy's room to tell him I was going away for the holidays. I gave him a hardcover copy of Tennyson's poetry as a Christmas gift.

I was taking a Tennyson course with a young professor who held classes in his apartment and who unnervingly confined his young wife to the bedroom when we young men were over. I had the feeling that he feared that one of us would run away with his Guinevere. We always had the captive's homemade baked goods to snack on while we discussed the darkest passages in Tennyson's work inspired by the curse of mental breakdowns, depression, uncontrolled rages, alcoholism and drug use in his family. It wasn't this part of Tennyson I wanted to share with Andy but instead his great poem of King Arthur's tale *Idylls of the King* which became as addicting for me as videogames are for young men today. This poem not only had knights and maidens, a wizard and a world-class villain, but it had hope as King Arthur tries to create a just order, a moral universe—The

Knights of the Roundtable. That he ultimately fails does not matter. As young as I was, I knew this poem reflected my age of Vietnam, civil rights and liberation from poisonous mores, but also the possibilities of a new and better world.

When Arthur is dying, Sir Belvedere, his marshall, cries out:

"Ah! my Lord Arthur, whither shall I go? Where shall I hide my forehead and my eyes?/For now I see the true old times are dead." Arthur replies, "The old order changeth, yielding place to new."

It was this hope I was giving Andy tucked into the binding of the book.

As for the poor professor's wife, as we read *Idylls*, I imagined that the professor would find one day that like Queen Guinevere, his wife "had fled the court, and sat/There in the holy house at Almesbury/Weeping, none with her save a little maid," at least until a Lancelot came along who didn't have her make cookies for over-privileged teenagers.

I next stopped by Tom's to say goodbye. I had to knock a few times because the music was loud and I could hear that he was jumping up and down. He was practicing.

The first time I saw Tom's small room, I was startled. It was a monk's cell with one exception. On six feet of one wall there was a floor-to-ceiling mirror and what, courtesy of my time unwillingly spent at Miss Enid Botsford's Ballroom Dancing and Etiquette classes, I knew to be a ballet barre.

"I was eleven," Tom told me the first time I found him in his shared kitchen in a white T-shirt and black tights. "I saw the Ed Sullivan show. There were these dancers. Ballet dancers. I couldn't get them out of my mind. I wanted to be the young man partnering the beautiful young woman. I had never seen a ballet before. Somehow, probably through the Yellow Pages, I found my way to the School of American Ballet on Madison. This was the feeder school for George Balanchine and the New York City Ballet and it was NYCB dancers it turns out that I saw on Ed Sullivan that night. I just hung around the School until they let me in and gave me free lessons. My father worked as a waiter at the Rainbow Room so he wasn't home evenings. I told my mother I was kept after school to help the teachers."

Tom was by now in a trance revisiting his creation myth. I hardly breathed.

"Eventually I told my parents. My father beat me. My mother cried. It was hard for my father, who fled Greece with my mother after the Italians invaded, to understand that after all his sacrifices, his son wanted to dance. But after they visited the School and met my teacher, a great old man, Pierre Vladimiroff, they understood better. The athleticism of those classes, the beautiful young women and the European gentility. Vladimir was a real character. He was once shot in the nose in a duel over a woman. My father liked his stories and they understood each other. Pierre was a political exile like Dad."

"I was allowed to continue. My folks paid what they could. I was in the yearly *Nutcracker*. I advanced quickly.

Mr. Balanchine noticed me. He said someday I would be in the corps. But I became interested in psychology and went to City College instead. I still take classes at the School, but it's different. The move to Lincoln Center has made a different animal. I take a class every week and sometimes I see Mr. Balanchine. He always shakes his head and says the same thing. "I could have made you a great dancer."

I left for Christmas, thinking how the rooms in the Van Cortlandt opened up like the windows in an Advent calendar.

Quite honestly, I actually had a self-serving motive in accepting Grant's invitation. I was always holding tryouts for new parents and interviewing my friends' parents to see how far I could insinuate myself into yet another family. Grant's parents fit my upscale aspirations nicely. His father was an international businessman. That had a good generic upscale sound to it. But I was interested in auditioning his mother. His mother was the daughter of the fourth-to-last Governor-General of the Belgian Congo. Grant adored her and told a wowser of a story about his grandfather taking his young family for a holiday to Lake Victoria. Grant's mother who was seven or eight had just gotten a small dog and was inseparable from it, so was allowed to take it along. When the family went out on a small pleasure boat on LV, the dog accompanied Grant's mother. A few hundred feet from shore, the dog saw something moving in the water and peeked over the side to investigate. A giant crocodile shot up from the still, dark lake, grabbed the screaming pooch and disappeared into a murky dog Hades. The family returned to shore at once.

Grant also invited Wu, who did not want to return to Hawaii for Christmas, and Ray, who had just lost his mother after losing his father the year before. We were a band of outsiders. Grant was assured of being the big man off campus.

I also had a cultural connection with Grant's mother. My freshman year, I brought a small black-and-white television with me to keep up on a soap opera I had been watching with my high school friends to prepare us for the real world. *Love of Life* began broadcasting in 1951 along with its sister shows *Search for Tomorrow* and *The Secret Storm*. These early television soap operas transferred a format from radio and were named "soaps" for the soap products that sponsored them. They were domestic operas with plots as improbable as *The Barber of Seville* or *Cosi fan tutte*. While a housewife washed, dried, folded, cooked and cleaned, she could watch these aspirational melodramas, set in the new suburbs and filled with well-dressed, well-coiffed characters who all had professional jobs that somehow allowed them to spend a lot of time murdering actors whose contracts had expired, swapping spouses, harboring secrets, succumbing to disease, being miraculously cured or exhibiting signs of schizophrenia, all without ultimate consequence to their lifestyles. And occasionally a vampire or space alien would show up.

Many of my high school friends thought our own suburb, Brighton, was the model for the *Love of Life* community of Rosehill and that somehow the unrepentant Nazi who tied the eternal heroine Vanessa to a chair in the basement of her house while setting the living room on fire to cover up evidence of his genocidal past had a cognate somewhere in our real-life town. We did everything we could to not miss an episode. Whenever one of us stayed home on sick leave, we'd arise from our death beds at the stroke of noon so we could report on the latest tragic development. We found a television in the music room at school that lay fallow and thanks to a young, tolerant music teacher, we spent as many lunch hours as we could deciphering Vanessa and her husband Dr. Bruce Sterling's complicated love of life.

You would think this would be a hard cultural translation to an all men's college. Not at all. By the second week of school, my roommates were rescheduling their classes. After the first month, we were hosting ten to twelve freshmen in our room who found Vanessa and Bruce a lot more relatable than Agamemnon and Clytemnestra, although the family histories were somewhat similar. And this is how I met Grant. He came into the *Love of Life* circle one day and called his empty nester mother up to tell her about his soap opera college experience. She had been hooked for a year by the time I was invited. Although she had never met me, she called me "John, ce jeune homme qui m'a accro à *L'amour de la vie*. In other words, I was in. A known and approved quantity.

Ipswich, Massachusetts became famous in 1968 as the real-life location of the community of Tarbox, a small town north of Boston which was the setting of John Updike's best-selling novel *Couples*, Updike's mod porn novel about the effect of the sexual revolution on ten Ipswichian couples. It's an upper-middle-class companion piece to Philip Roth's lower-middle-class *Portnoy's Complaint* and Gore Vidal's intersex fantasia *Myra Breckenridge*.

And wouldn't you know that Tarbox, I mean Ipswich, is where Grant's parents lived. *Love of Life* in real-time.

Grant's mother greeted the four of us at the train station in a predictable wood-paneled station wagon. After kissing her son, greeting all of us, she interrogated me. Did I really think Vanessa was schizophrenic and could she possibly have ax-murdered old Doctor Robertson? Grant shifted uncomfortably. Ray, who was a solid engineer type and had been Grant's freshman roommate, remained silent. I was clearly the expert in the station wagon. I liked her, a lot, and not only for the attention I was getting. She was an upper class European but did not have the frosty reserve I expected. She was a mother. Her husband was in Asia and not coming back for Christmas. She was openly appreciative of the guests her son had brought. And she clearly loved Grant.

We reached the house which was a carefully remodeled early 19th-century Georgian home—large not grand, plain spoken yet elegant. The house suited its ménage.

We unpacked the groceries she had bought for Christmas dinner and then she told Grant we were on our own for this one evening since she was driving up to Boston to spend the night with her best friend who had just come out of life-threatening surgery. It was a Christmas promise she made before she knew we were coming. She would be back the next morning in time to make Christmas Eve dinner. She had already made us a variety of foods and she and Grant exchanged a rapid inventory of dishes and preparations in French. After this, Grant chided her for leaving, or so I gathered, but again in French so as not to directly engage us. I was pretty sure he was telling her that a blizzard was forecast and that she shouldn't leave because she might not be able to return. There were a few dismissive gestures on her part. Grant's mother didn't survive the Congo and World War II to let a snowstorm keep her from a dying friend.

After showing us our bedrooms, she left.

A library, a mysterious spiral staircase to the attic, a lot of 19th-century paintings and some family portraits gave definition to the house. Grant pointed out two very valuable Congolese carvings currently being used as end tables.

Grant insisted we put our coats and boots back on to go out to the garage. His future twenty-first birthday gift was there. I assumed he wanted to show us a Volkswagen or perhaps a Citroen that would become his upon graduation. Instead, he opened the garage door on a 1952 Rolls Royce Silver Dawn with a full bar with Waterford decanters. It didn't run, Grant said, but he was going to have it repaired and take it to Manhattan. He intended to rent himself out as a Wall Street chauffeur to junior partners who wanted to make an early, inexpensive impression on their bosses.

Around six o'clock we started to forage. As we ate our pre-prepared dinner, it began to snow. And it snowed. And it snowed. And it snowed.

Grant's mother called. It was snowing too hard to drive back from Boston. She lamented that she would stay with her friend.

And it snowed through the night.

By morning, when it was still snowing, we realized that we were in the house for the day. I don't know when any of us had been housebound without transportation before. The useless Silver Dawn sat in the garage in rebuke.

Grant made us breakfast. He liked to cook. Afterward, we confronted the fact that we were really four young strangers stuck in a large house on Christmas Eve with no gifts and nothing to do. There were no computers, no social media, no cell phones. And speaking of phones, the house phone was now dead.

It snowed some more.

We turned on the television which was in the kitchen, black-and-white and as small as mine. We watched *The Today Show* and *Concentration*. There was a brief dust-up when it came time to decide between *Love of Life* and *Hollywood Squares*. Ray, as a pragmatic engineer, was not a fan of soap operas. He didn't give a shit about Vanessa. My argument was about tradition and respecting Grant's mother's viewing habits. We watched *Hollywood Squares*.

Ray and Grant played chess. Wu was in a window seat reading Timothy Leary's *High Priest*. I looked out the large dining room window and through the blizzard, I thought I saw a horse.

"I think I see a horse," I said. This roused everyone. Soon we all saw a horse.

As the horse approached, we also made out the shadow of an upright rider covered in snow. "Oh, it's Bob Robertson," Grant said. Robert Robertson, a WASP prank, I thought.

Grant went out into the snowdrifts to greet him. Mr. Robertson dismounted, tied his horse to something arbitrary and walked into the kitchen looking like a character from an Anthony Mann western.

He looked at Ray, Wu and me uncomprehendingly.

"Where's your mother?" he asked in a gnarled Yankee accent.

"She's stuck in Boston," Grant replied.

"I came to see if she was alright." Alright was swallowed into one syllable.

I had a flash that Grant's mother had been paying closer attention to the plotlines of *Love of Life* than I thought.

"Now are you OK? Got enough food? This is going on for two more days." Grant assured him of our ability to survive with a full refrigerator ten feet away.

Robertson left.

We found a game of Monopoly. Grant and Ray unsuccessfully tried to teach me to play poker. We cooked the food that had been left for us, watched *Green Acres*, and then at 9:30 p.m. along with one out of every four people on the planet, watched Apollo 8 circumnavigate the moon.

Wu continued to read *High Priest* and complained that he had forgotten his tabs of acid.

After Commander Frank Boorman described the moon as "a vast, lonely, forbidding expanse of nothing," each astronaut took turns reading from the Book of Genesis. Live from the orbit of the moon,

Astronaut William Anders read:

> *"For all the people on Earth the crew of Apollo 8 has a message we would like to send you."*
>
> *"In the beginning God created the heaven and the earth.*
>
> *And the earth was without form, and void; and darkness was upon the face of the deep.*
>
> *And the Spirit of God moved upon the face of the waters. And God said, Let there be light: and there was light.*
>
> *And God saw the light, that it was good: and God divided the light from the darkness."*

And then Astronaut Jim Lovell read:

> *"And God called the light Day, and the darkness he called Night. And the evening and the morning were the first day.*
>
> *And God said, Let there be a firmament in the midst of the waters, and let it divide the waters from the waters.*

> *And God made the firmament, and divided the waters which were under the firmament from the waters which were above the firmament: and it was so.*
>
> *And God called the firmament Heaven. And the evening and the morning were the second day."*

And then Frank Borman:

> *"And God said, Let the waters under the heavens be gathered together unto one place, and let the dry land appear: and it was so.*
>
> *And God called the dry land Earth; and the gathering together of the waters called the Seas: and God saw that it was good."*

Borman signed off with "And from the crew of Apollo 8, we close with good night, good luck, a Merry Christmas, and God bless all of you - all of you on the good Earth."

After the broadcast, I breathed a sigh of relief. They had used the *King James* version.

Chapter Eight

On Christmas Day, the phone still did not work. Grant fretted about his mother, but we assured him she was safe and sleeping in a hospital chair somewhere. Maybe.

Ray, who had already made some small repairs to the house, was intrigued by the spiral staircase that led to the attic. With Grant's permission, Ray ascended.

After about 20 minutes, Ray tripped down the spiral and asked Grant, "What does your father do?"

"He's an importer/exporter. Before that he was a journalist," Grant replied.

"He's no importer/exporter," Ray smugly returned. "He's a spy. Come on up, I'll show you."

Three of us went up like two Hardy Boys with a cousin. Wu stayed downstairs still plumbing Timothy Leary's depths. Ray took us over to a few small containers, the kind that hold four gallons of milk. One was filled with about ten small silver cameras; one had tape recorder parts, and one had some upended shoe boxes. Ray picked up one. "Look inside," he directed Grant. There were some press passes and underneath those were three passports: American, Belgian and British. That would have been plausible if the three passports which had identical photos were issued in the same name. These weren't. Three different passports, three different names. All with a handsome photo of Grant's father.

"Spy," Ray the empirical thinker repeated.

"Businessman," Grant insisted with hesitation.

"Spy," Ray countered.

"Investigative journalist," Grant shot back.

"Where?"

"Rome. *Rome Daily American*."

Thirty years later I came across an article about the *Rome Daily American*. Yes, it was owned by the C.I.A.

Grant's mother came back the day after Christmas on horseback. More specifically on the back of Mr. Robertson's horse with Mr. Robertson still on it. Vanessa would have been proud of this plot development. She went to work being a mom, made us more food and kept up a bright chatter. But the mood had been broken; she had missed Christmas. No mention was made of her sick friend.

Grant too soured on the holiday. Ray had broken the spell of friendship. Grant's father was now implicated as a very un-Sixties tool of the establishment. Even Wu had difficulty being his smooth self. He hadn't dropped acid for three days and was increasingly irritable that he had missed tripping during the televised view of the heavens.

I said goodbye and took a bus to Rochester. I was happy to be going home.

Back in Rochester, I fell into the comfortable camaraderie of my friends. The Group, we called ourselves, with a conscious nod to Mary McCarthy. The few younger members were now also in college, which was a great leveler. But there was precious little to do since we were unmoored in our hometown. We drank little and did no drugs. We mainly went from one dysfunctional household to another. We had all successfully escaped, yet we all came back to do time voluntarily.

The local paper ran a feature on Ingrid Bergman's brief season in Rochester when she lived in my hometown with her husband, dental surgeon Petter Lindstrom. I had to agree with her assessment of her time here while she was a pre-*Casablanca* doctor's wife: "Rochester was a quiet, plain city and it was wrong for me to have expected more. But for me it was unbearably dull with nothing to do."

Bill and I did go see "Skidoo," Otto Preminger's forlorn attempt at making an LSD movie that inexplicably starred Carol Channing, probably the least countercultural figure in the history of art. I thought of Wu and his 300 acid trips. Otto could have used him as a consultant. The movie was at the old Paramount, one of three movie palaces that still kept the downtown alive. Its worn elegance was quite a change from 42nd Street. And no one was selling ice cream in the aisles.

I bought underwear for a return to college and watched *The Ed Sullivan Show* Sunday night with my parents, who were mesmerized by the triple threat of Eddie Albert, Lainie Kazan and Judy Collins. I can still hear Ed introducing Collins with, "Now something for the young people in our audience," while the camera focused on the one young person who was paid to be in the audience.

I thought a lot about Barbara Jane Mackle, a young woman who had just been dug up alive near Atlanta where a kidnapper had buried her in a shallow grave. The headline read: **Coed Found Unharmed in Box Buried in Woods North of Atlanta**. I sympathized. Air was running out in my own box north of Atlanta.

I rang in the New Year with The Group at a back table at Howard Johnson's. We were all home by twelve fifteen.

On New Year's Day, I called Evie. Her father answered and was rather abrupt with me. When Evie came to the phone, it was clear she had been crying. "You didn't call me for New Year's Eve," she pouted. "I'm sorry. It never occurred to me," I said, because it hadn't.

"I never want to see you again," she said as she hung up. And she never did.

It was pretty easy being a cad.

I took a night plane back to the City and after wintry delays ended up back at The Club very late. The door was open to the corridor rooms so, having propeller plane lag and excited to be out of the dead zone, I decided to see if anyone was up. I passed by the shared bathroom. The door was wide open, the light on. The shower curtain had been ripped from the rod. It was covering something. As I approached, I realized it was a body. A not-so-young male. White. With a winter jacket on. His eyes were open and his lips were blue.

I continued on to Tom's room and knocked on the door. After several internal grumbles, Tom opened it.

"There's a body in your bathtub," I coolly informed him, especially for someone who had only seen bodies in home funeral parlors, all with their eyes closed.

After several "huhs," Tom accompanied me to the morbid bathroom.

"Holy cow!" he said. Tom never swore.

And then he swiveled around looking for someone else to bear witness, to help.

There was no one else. Not a creature was stirring except Tom and me.

"I guess I should call the police," I said.

"Yes. Yes. I'll stay here to warn people."

Of course, there was no one on duty in the cage at two in the morning and the super didn't answer his bell.

So I decided to call the police from the trusty Amsterdam Avenue phone booth. That summer, the City began using the 911 system and I was well prepared by billboards and phone booth stickers to try it out.

But first, I walked by the fire station at the end of 113th. A month before, late at night, when I was returning to the Club, a fireman popped out of the station with the requisite Dalmatian and said, "Young man, did you ever think of joining the Fire Department? Good pay. Good benefits. And lots of time to read," he added, acknowledging my student status.

This same fireman was sitting in an open bay.

"Hi," I greeted him

"Change your mind?" he inquired.

"No," I said. "Sorry. "I'm afraid of heights. I have a problem though. There's a body in the Van Cortlandt."

"Dead?" he cautiously asked.

"I'm pretty sure," I cautiously answered.

"Third one so far this month."

He sprang to action, roused his firefighting colleagues. They hopefully collected life-saving equipment and we sprinted to sprint toward the Van Cortlandt.

Once there, they followed me up the stairs, down the hallway, down the corridor.

I briefly introduced them to Tom who had been standing guard lest someone come to use the bathroom.

"Yeah, he's dead all right. Overdose."

It was only then I noticed the rubber hose and the syringe.

They called the police on their walkie-talkies and soon the corridor was filled with people. Tenants. Police. Firefighters. Someone brought a body bag. Someone else a stretcher. A board was nailed up across the bathroom awaiting the arrival of detectives. This was an era before yellow police line tape, so the bathroom merely looked condemned.

"Where in the hell am I going to go to the toilet?" someone I had never seen before complained.

Soon all was back to normal. The next morning, I awoke when Andy knocked on my door. "For some reason there's a board nailed across the bathroom door. I have to pee."

Happy that he wasn't peeing in bottles, I welcomed him. When he emerged from the bathroom, I told him of the night's events. He had slept right through them.

Chapter Nine

No one came to talk to me about the corpse in the bathtub, yet the board with a crime scene warning remained nailed across the bathroom door, meaning that Tom, Andy and I shared my bathroom for several days.

On Tuesday, a young couple who lived in a corridor room knocked on my door and asked to use my bathroom. I knew them by sight but not by name. They introduced themselves as Theo and Angel. They were quintessential flower children. Theo always wore shiny fake leather pants and a velvet jacket over a seen-better-days ruffled white shirt. Angel wore a rainbow sundress and a floppy straw hat that partly covered her eyes. In winter. They were Americana, 1969.

After the introductions, Theo and Angel went into my bathroom together. And they stayed there a long time. Ten minutes. Fifteen minutes. A half-hour. Forty-five minutes. I read. I opened and closed the refrigerator. I clanked kitchenware. I cleared my throat. I coughed vigorously. To no effect. When they finally emerged, they just walked to the door and left without saying a word.

I went into the bathroom because now I had reason to. There was blood in the sink. There was blood on the floor. There was blood on the towels provided and changed weekly by Clarabelle.

I went to find Tom and brought him back to witness the bloodletting.

"Crap," Tom said because he never swore. "This place is turning into a shooting gallery." A lightbulb went off probably from my reading Nelson Algren the year before. Theo and Angel were DRUG ADDICTS!

"Clean this up with rubber gloves on. Use my bathroom."

We walked down the corridor to the bathroom the corpse had resided in. Tom ripped off the loosely attached board and crumpled up the crime warning. "No one's come back so to hell with them," Tom emphatically declared. Tom never swore.

I used the dead man's bathroom.

I must admit I was a little bit lonely. My options for female companionship were limited, so I started hanging out with Pat. You may recall Andy and I had watched the Horowitz concert on her small black-and-white television.

Pat called me her little brother. It was a title I accepted with honor.

Pat lived in a room in the other corridor on the floor. She had been a Southern Belle from Tennessee who had wanted independence and adventure. She said she was 35 but she was too out of focus for even 45. No matter. She was enchanting. She had the gift of gab, of narrative, of metaphor, of simile, of the whole toolbox of language. She told stories about her family that could go on for miles and then would come to an abrupt stop when she would start crying so hard her mascara would disintegrate. "I'll never see any of them again. I can't let them see me like this" was the classic punctuation she would use when telling tales of forbidden love, unrequited love, requited love with tragic results and familial hate. Her Tennessee was like Faulkner's Mississippi—an endless stream of invention. You could put your hand in the stream any time and catch five stories.

Pat chose the local bar, Jim's, to cast her spells. It was an old-fashioned bar. It wasn't a pick-up bar, although Pat was not unavailable; it wasn't a gay bar; it wasn't a honky-tonk bar; it wasn't a hipster bar like the famous West End down the street. It was just a bar. You hung out. You drank. You told stories. You walked out into the night with your lonely life as your only companion.

Pat was a secretary who worked as a temp. At about ten every night, she would leave Jim's and go back to her room. She had insomnia so she would spend hours after midnight shaping and reshaping an army of men. Pat made soft sculptures of ideal mates. They were completely featureless and had no genitalia, but to her they were men who could love her. There were about twenty of them piled around her small room. When she made a new one out of pillowcases, foam and rope, she would convene a naming committee. Tom, Andy and I had each sat on several. She liked ordinary masculine names like Bob or Jerry or Hank. Once when I suggested Aloysius she berated me. She would then make up romantic stories of her adventures with Bob or Jerry or Hank. Schoolgirl stories. Dates and dances. Proposals. Flowers received. Flirtations. Dinners out. Real honest-to-God Blanche DuBois stuff. The committee would sit there, applaud and choose the best mate based on the best story.

Even then in the full-blown ignorance of youth, I knew Pat was one of the bravest people I had ever encountered. She taught me that life was a series of stories and if you divided it as such, you could survive anything. Like Scheherazade.

A few winter weeks after I returned, Bill came down for a day. He had been visiting his ex-girlfriend in New Paltz.

At Duke's Diner at 110th and Broadway, which I preferred to Tom's, he told me that his older brother Eric was going to come to New York to try to break into modeling and he needed a place to stay for a few weeks until he got a place of his own.

I looked at him blankly.

"He'll pay half the rent."

At that point I got it. Eric? Live with Eric? It would be like living with . . . I then reviewed a list of insane barbaric rulers throughout history and came up with . . . Attila the Hun.

"He's changed."

"Oh, you mean he won't make fun of me anymore?"

"He probably will, but he said he always liked you."

This was highly improbable. Eric was the most famous non-graduate in the history of our high school. He was an amalgamation of James Dean and Marlon Brando with a pheromone count in the billions. He looked like an early template for The Terminator. Aryan. Aryan. Aryan. With the skin of a peach and the smile of an executioner.

He was also fearless.

His most notorious exploit was brutal in its simplicity. One legendary day, our jock high school principal, Mr. Carlson, stopped him in the halls and told him that his hair was too long. Carlson told him to come back when he had gotten a haircut. Eric, obeying the letter of the law, came back two hours later with a Mohawk. A dyed red Mohawk. No suburban kid even knew what a Mohawk was then. We all took turns going by Carlson's office to see this bright red spike that ran down Eric's head. When Mr. Carlson opened his office door and saw Eric, he flipped out. He started screaming that Eric could come back to school when he had a full head of hair again. Eric came back an hour later wearing a Beatles' wig.

If you wanted a teacher's car keyed or someone hoisted up the flagpole or ball bearings released during girls' gym class, Eric was your guy. But he wasn't a hood. He read

Sartre and Wittgenstein, neither of whom managed to keep him from being expelled.

Eric's father, also Bill's father, threw him out of the house at this juncture, so at seventeen Eric signed on to a merchant ship, jumped when it got to Marseille, bought a BMW motorcycle and drove it across Central Asia. In 1966 So, of course, I said sure. "When does he want to move in?"

"Tomorrow," Bill replied.

Chapter Ten

"Don't touch my stuff. Don't touch my food. Don't touch my toiletries. Don't touch me." These were the first words my new roommate directed toward me as he brought in three large duffel bags of clothes that took up most of the middle of the room.

I had done an obligatory introduction to Ms. Dutto earlier and her usual cage rage melted as Eric directed a sociopath's smile in her direction. "We're so happy to have you here at the Van Cortlandt in our family. I'm sure you'll keep Mr. Borek in line. If you need anything just come right down and ask me personally." You could see her bosom heave.

Eric spent most of his time ironing. One duffel bag contained nothing but Gant shirts. It is impossible to overstate the popularity of Gant dress shirts in the Sixties. People conflate Sixties clothing with fringe, leather and flower power polyester fabrics. But young men on the move wore 100% cotton Gant shirts that were usually white or light pastels. They had button-down collars and a little tab on the back of the shirt so you could hang it up in a locker and still keep the creases pure. This gave them an extra varsity dimension. Stylish, but manly.

When Eric left in the morning for his round of modeling auditions, he looked the personification of cool. He often wore double denim—jeans and a denim jacket. These were lightly frayed. He turned himself into a poster boy for the soulful young man of the era, straddling the Beats and the Hippies. And it worked. His first day out, he got a modeling contract for a book cover. He was paid $500 to sit for an illustrator for two days. When I asked him to pay his share of the rent, he yelled at me about what a shithole my room was.

I lived with King Eric for four months. I introduced him to my Van Cortlandt family and he greeted each with a demeaning, intolerant smile. He sure had lipsful of caustic smiles at his disposal. His opinion of them was more than caustic. It was searing. He never referred to any of them by their names. Andy was "the fruitcake," Tom was "twinkle toes" and Pat was "that hag."

In the morning, getting ready for classes, he often locked me out of the bathroom, making me use a bathroom in one of the corridors. Eric had a ninety-minute bathroom regimen during which I imagine he opened and closed his pores one at a time. He appropriated the only shelf with an abundance of goat milk soap from Alaska, shea butter and jojoba oil. There was also a beautiful hand-lettered note on cardboard that said Do Not Touch followed by his signature.

I was not allowed to have visitors and whenever his girlfriend visited I was like Mama next door. I had to make myself scarce while the deed was done. Any protest was greeted with a string of expletives followed by a threat of physical violence.

I suffered in silence and prayed for the day he would tire of my shithole.

Michael was at Smilers buying a sandwich. He had been my Humanities professor the year before. The professor/student barrier all but collapsed during the riots, so after the semester was suspended, he continued to hold classes in his apartment which was in a Columbia-owned expansive ten-story building on 125th and Riverside.

When I saw Michael, I had this idea. I mostly wanted someone to exorcise the very real demon in my apartment. Michael was a veteran of the Korean War and had received a Purple Heart, even though he said he was only shot in the ass. He was physically imposing and larger than Eric. I knew that Eric could not sneer at Michael and could not mock him. If anything, it would work the other way. Perhaps we could reset new boundaries. Michael could break the ban on visitors. I invited Michael to see my new digs and meet my roommate. Reciprocity for hosting classes.

Around the corner. Into the Van Cortland and up the winding stairs behind the elevator. I opened the door to my large room. Eric was in the bathroom scrubbing his face, getting ready for another photoshoot.

Eric did not acknowledge our presence and after a few more minutes of grooming, came out and asked if I didn't remember our agreement. By agreement, he meant, of course, no visitors.

"I'm John's professor. Do you have a problem with that? Or maybe you were never in college. I'll give you a dollar for your college fund." And with that he took a dollar out of his wallet and threw it toward Eric. It floated slowly to the floor.

Eric sneered, grabbed his modeling kit and left, slamming the door shut and stomping all the way to the elevator.

I was sure I would pay for this later. But for now, my plan had worked.

"Who was THAT?" Michael asked. "My friend's brother. I thought it would be, well, nice to have a roommate. He wanted to break into modeling, so I told him if he paid half the rent he could stay here. But . . . it wasn't such a good idea."

"His girlfriend's coming Friday. That's when I'll spend the night watching movies on 42nd Street."

"Huh?"

"Yeah, he asks me to leave when Lulu visits. I catch up on movies."

"On 42nd Street?"

"It's not bad. They all have double features. They run a lot of Hawks and Ford and Sam Fuller."

Michael lit a cigarette and blew the smoke straight up. We were at the kitchen table at the back window, nowhere near the kitchen. He was contemplating my junk tree view through my grimy window. I'm sure he was thinking like me about how vulnerable I was with the fire escape right outside my window. And with Eric inside.

After a long, thought-filled pause, Michael said: "When I was 17," he started, slowly, "I got a girl pregnant. She had a boy and being a good girl she put him up for adoption. He would be just about your age now."

I was respectfully quiet.

"Why don't you stay at my mother's Friday night. She lives on the East Side."

I thought for less than a second about abandoning the grindhouse for a night. The drunks, the junkies, the ice cream vendors walking up and down the theater aisles. And I never went up into the balconies. That was Sodom and Gomorrah.

"Sure," I said. And I thought maybe I am his son.

Chapter Eleven

Michael had written down the address and his mother's phone number. I decided to walk. I often walked instead of taking the subway. Cabs were out of the question. The address was a nice round number. 1000 Park Avenue.

Dinner was at 7. I left at 5 and arrived an hour early. I had my little wallet address calculator card so I knew I was going to either 84th or 85th Street. Drop the 0 on 1000; divide by 2; add 35 for Park Avenue. There was nowhere to wait and I was cold so I spent about 45 minutes in the church across the street—St. Ignatius Loyola. To give you some idea of the neighborhood, in later years Jacqueline Kennedy Onassis, Philip Seymour Hoffman and Mario Cuomo all had their funerals there.

A doorman greeted me under the building's canopy. I told him I was going to dinner at Mrs. Moore's. As he rang up my hostess, I tried to make sense of the Gothic sculptures that flanked the building. One resembled a medieval gnome that appeared to hold the Parthenon.

There was an elevator operator. I stole a look at myself in the mirror. My hair was too long for this building, but my tie was straight.

A maid opened the door. Already the staff was as large as my family. I was ushered into a comfortable study lined with exotic wood bookcases and Sister Parrish furniture although I wouldn't know about Sister Parrish or pre-war New York apartment buildings for several decades. I had brought a small vagrant suitcase which the maid took from my hand.

Michael's mother came in. Although I had never seen anyone other than the Marx Brother's foil Margaret Dumont who looked even vaguely like her, she was nobody's mark. She glided into the room, took my hand in hers and at the same time scared me and put me at ease. "You're Michael's student. How lovely to meet you. Would you like something to drink?" Scotch was the right answer, but I asked for a Coke. "Mary, could you bring John a soft drink?"

She asked me about myself and I started talking about my unformed life, leaving out recent lurid details. She inquired after my parents, my schooling and asked if Michael was a good teacher.

And then Mary beckoned us for dinner. Mary opened the doors to the dining room and suddenly I was in Peking, 1910.

Pagoda-red bibelots, black lacquer furniture, precise rosewood carvings, silk panels with a variety of birds from the Phoenix to the peacock, a huge blue rug with an enormous red Chinese character in the middle and vases of silk poppies commingled with real flowers that I could not name. You could not find a more beautiful room at the Metropolitan Museum. The table was set with Oriental porcelain. Two places. No one would be joining us for dinner. A command performance.

I had run out of personal anecdotes. But I needn't have been concerned. As the soup came and went, as the meat course was carved and served, as the desert tray floated by, Mrs. Moore talked. It was her command performance.

I commented on the room. How could I not? She was born in China, she said. Her parents were Protestant missionaries. Some things in the room were her mother's, but most of the room was assembled on her return trips. She was interested in the plight of women in China and worked diligently to improve their lives. I got a comprehensive rundown on everything from foot binding to widow chastity, from arranged marriages to concubines, from the Song to the Ming to the Qing dynasties. It ended with a story about her friend Pearl Buck. I nodded in exhaustion at about 9:30 and she sent me off with Mary to a small but comfortable and elegant guest room with linen sheets I now assume to be Irish. I took my collected Tennyson out of my suitcase and I fell asleep reading Tennyson's poem Ulysses. By the time I read

I am a part of all that I have met;
Yet all experience is an arch wherethro'
Gleams that untravell'd world whose margin fades
For ever and forever when I move.

I was asleep.

I awoke late. I could hear the muffled sounds of the household through the thick pre-war walls. I quickly showered and shaved in my private bath and made my way down the long corridor that connected one *Town and Country* room after another.

When I got to the kitchen I saw Michael, who was having a cup of coffee and a cigarette. "I got a call from my friend Bob Natkin. He wants to show me his new painting. Wanna come along?"

I nodded in assent and looked sideways at the tiered hard-boiled eggs server that displayed cooked eggs with shells on them. My mother had always removed the shells. How did you eat such creatures?

After breakfast, I packed my vagrant suitcase. I said goodbye to Mary. We left and walked to Michael's fancy foreign car. I had only been in repurposed Volkswagens and Peugeots. I didn't even know what kind it was.

We drove to the west and then down, down, down the old Westside Highway. We got off somewhere with a lot of warehouses and no people. It was Saturday and this was still blue-collar New York. No workday. No people. We got out in front of the warehouses and took a freight elevator up several floors.

When we stepped off the elevator I saw what I regarded then as an old man with a shock of white hair dressed in the kind of white overalls that house painters wear. He had on a Sherwin Williams cap. If he stood still, you could read the

Sherwin-Williams slogan "We cover the world." The manic way he was painting made that entirely possible.

Natkin was an action painter like Pollack and de Kooning. His canvases received paint as benedictions, violent gestures or caresses. He used kitchen sponges or other soft-textured and absorbent objects he dipped in various pots of mostly pastel paints and daubed or slammed them against the canvases.

Michael greeted him, but I'm not sure Natkin acknowledged us. He was too busy getting paint on his canvases and himself. Around this time he was a hot commodity. In a decade or so he would even have an Abrams art book monograph. The particular painting he was attacking this morning was very beautiful, but I'm not sure beauty is much of an asset in modernity.

We stayed for about an hour. Michael and Natkin occasionally exchanged words but not many. Natkin lit up a cigar and Michael a cigarette. There were a lot of paint thinners around. I imagined three charred bodies in front of the majestic unharmed canvas. I was relieved when we left.

Today Natkin is not on the Wiki list of notable action painters. Instead, he is largely remembered for licking a Vermeer at the Frick to get to know it better.

As Michael was driving me back to the Club, he said, "Thank you for having dinner with my mother."

"I enjoyed it," I replied but I meant, "I survived it."

"She had a tough week," he continued, "and I thought you'd cheer her up. And you did. This week my brother...." His voice trailed off.

When it's bad, he . . ." and then he trailed off again.

I knew not to ask for details.

Instead I said: "Why?" while wondering, not for the first or last time, how someone with everything could have nothing.

"Well, let's just say that when your first real girlfriend is Grace Kelly and when you go on a double date it's with Elizabeth Taylor and Conrad Hilton's kid, it's all downhill from there."

I was out of my league. I handed back my adoption papers.

It may have been a few months or a few years later when I found out that Mrs. Moore was Henry Luce's sister. Henry Luce's name doesn't mean much today, but even then in the late Sixties, the founder of *Time* and *Fortune* magazines was Steve Jobs, Bill Gates and Jeff Bezos all rolled up into one. Henry and his sister's childhoods in China had given him a window into the hunger for internationalism that would consume American news, culture and business for the whole of the 20th century. The Mrs. Moore I saw was equally accomplished but less visible. She became the first women President of the State University of New York system and headed the enormous Henry Luce Foundation. She had a string of philanthropic accomplishments that underscored her commitment to women, to education and to Asia.

Once, twenty years later, Mrs. Moore appeared at the University of Rochester to deliver a lecture on Women and Philanthropy. I attended the lecture. The audience was composed of elderly widows whose husbands had left them well-off and young progressive women who were graduate students and untenured faculty. She was treated quite maliciously by the young progressives in the audience who called her out for her privilege, the security of her position and, to them, her unearned status. It was clear that she had been through this before. A gracious mask greeted their sardonic questions. And she never for a moment revealed her early life that made their malice so empty. She could have spoken about what her family of missionaries had lived through: the vigilantes, the house burnings, the drownings of baby girls, the execution of beloved servants.

The young progressives had mistaken the present for the past.

I had brought her some flowers and a modest box of chocolates. I was so embarrassed by her treatment that I tried to exit without being noticed. As I walked behind her, she turned and said, "Why, John, how nice of you to come. How are you and your wife?" I stammered a reply, gave her the flowers and the chocolate. She disappeared into a cloud of ladies from local clubs.

Eric eventually moved out, taking his facial cleansing station and ironing board with him. Imagine my stunned surprise when I found a note from him under my door inviting me to his new place in the Village. I called him from the trusty Amsterdam Avenue pay phone and we arranged to meet at the restaurant on the first floor of his building, The Pink Teacup.

Chapter Twelve

The Village terrified me. It was filled with unmoored young people not following a professional path. Earlier that year, my father's secret and secretive business partner gave me a gift certificate to Barney's, the upscale clothing emporium, then on Seventh and Seventeenth. He instructed me to buy a suit. Instead, I bought two pair of the world's most expensive bell-bottoms. One pair was made from heavy white painter's pants material and highlighted with very narrow red and blue stripes the exact colors of our flag. This would be appropriate for protests and marches I thought. The second pair was made of an incredibly velvety British corduroy in an orange the color of, well, an orange.

They were so fashionable that they needed to be hemmed and fitted. I went to the fitting area and a guy not much older than me asked me to step into the cubicle for measurements. I stepped on an elevated carpeted circle and he went to work with pins in his mouth and wandering hands. After shifting several times during the two fittings to avoid his touching my testicles, he was finished and had no more pins left in his mouth. "What are you doing tonight?" he asked.

"Meeting my girlfriend," I truthfully answered, since it was still the Evie era.

"Pity," he replied.

It took me a decade of occasional reflection to get it.

I've always found cluelessness to be a virtue.

All this by way of saying that these pants were my Village uniform. No matter that when I walked around the Village young men struggling to stay upright in doorways would snarl at me and mutter "weekend hippie." I reveled like a Fauntleroy that my bell bottoms didn't come from some cheap clothing store on St. Marks Place.

I chose the flag pinstripes for dinner with Eric. This I felt would at least make a sartorial statement against his pressed Gant shirt.

I got off at Sheridan Square, and because I was a bit early went into the bookstore there. I can use the word eponymous here, I think. It was the Sheridan Square Bookstore.

I realize now that the Sheridan Square was the first real bookstore I ever was in. By real, I mean it didn't have books primarily for classes like the uptown college bookstore Salters or a few racks of books to cater to the mostly men who were not interested in greeting cards. It also wasn't filled with upscale framed medieval sheet music and glass showcased Egyptian plunder like Brentanos. It didn't have the acreage of remainders like Marlborough in Times Square. It had small poetry books with black and white covers, self-published mimeoed books of poetry, chapbooks, meditation pamphlets, books on Buddhism, crystals, a stack of *Be Here Now*s and *Whole Earth Catalog*s, Nicholas von Hoffman's *We Are the People Our Parents Warned Us Against*, vintage, (that is a year old) Louis Abolafia nudist presidential candidate posters, Abie Hoffman's *Revolution for the Hell of It*, Jean Rhys, Richard Brautigan's *Trout Fishing in America*, paperback book imprints like Bard and Mentor and Signet, *Been Down So lt Long It Looks Like Up To Me* by the dead-at-thirty-one Richard Farina, Tom Wolfe (even though he beat up on youth culture), Allen Ginsberg, *The Strawberry Statement* by that notorious Columbia student, Kerouac from *On the Road* to *Dharma Bums*, Edward Abbey's *Desert Solitaire* and *Sand County Almanac*, Che Guevara, Lawrence Ferlinghetti, Hunter Thompson's *Hell's Angels*, *The Harrad Experiment*, John Lennon's *In His Own Write,* Joan Baez's *Daybreak*, *Soul on Ice*, Burroughs' *Junkie, Naked Lunch, The Soft Machine* and *The Ticket That Exploded, Last Exit to Brooklyn,* Ken Kesey's anthems for the counterculture *One Flew Over the Cuckoo's Nest* and *Some Times a Great Notion*, John McPhee's *The Pine Barrens*, Black Sparrow Press, D.H. Lawrence, City Lights, Rochelle Owens, John Fante, Evelyn Waugh, *The Bell Jar*, Vonnegut, *Catch 22*, *A Clockwork Orange*, Celine, *The Crying of Lot 49, No Exit, Tropic of Cancer, Ulysses, In the Heart of the Country*, Kafka, *Stranger in a Strange Land*, Beckett, *The Second Sex*, Camus, *Franny and Zooey*, Camus, *Labyrinths, Our Lady of* *the Flowers*, Alexander Trocchi, Muriel Spark, *Siddartha and Steppenwolf*—the Herman Hesse twins, Wittgenstein, *City of Lights, The Feminine Mystique*, Kate Chopin, *Vindication of the Rights of Women, The Yellow Wallpaper, A Room of One's Own, Their Eyes Were Watching God.*

You know. A bookstore.

I asked the young man at the counter if there were any clerk openings and after he responded with a weary no, I bought a copy of the *East Village Other*, a counterculture tabloid whose newsprint seemed thinner than tissue paper. I was late. I walked quickly down West 4th feeling that with the *Other* tucked under my arm like a businessman would tuck *The Wall Street Journal*, I gave a good impression of belonging Downtown.

I found the Pink Teacup. In an era of general urban scuzziness, the Teacup won the prize. The white exterior had a decade of the City's grime on it; the pink interior was a ghetto paint job—the kind you'd hire addicts to do in 30 minutes for a free meal. Cracks, light switches, moldings were all smothered in lumpy pink paint. The kitchen was separated from the diners by a dirty shower curtain covered in a seashell print. How could the food not be good? The overall effect was that of stumbling upon a gem of a restaurant in the back alleys of Cuzco.

I was late but Eric was nowhere in sight. I ordered a Coke, was given a menu too large for a small space and unfolded *The Other*. After spending 15 minutes reading letters from distraught parents begging their missing children to come home, ads for encounter sessions which girls could attend for free, a review of H. Rap Brown's Die ***** Die by Abie Hoffman, and the obligatory screed on how alternative radio station WBAI wasn't what it used to be, Eric appeared.

Eric had changed his look. He now wore a workman's blue shirt and painter's pants. Some things never change, however. Both shirt and pants were spotless and perfectly pressed. He unexpectedly said he was paying for dinner. In shock, I ordered salmon croquettes because my mother made them. I was uncomfortable navigating collards, grits, sweet potato waffles and cornbread. Eric ordered catfish. I had never heard of catfish.

It transpired that Lulu had left him. I suspected he had no one to show off his new life in the Village to so he had to stoop to his younger brother's friend. And I was probably the total of his friends. In the four months we lived in the same room, I never met a single friend of his. I finally concluded there were none.

Eric was now a carpenter. He earned more money than modeling for book covers. He had used his new skills to renovate his tenement apartment which he insisted showing me after dinner since it was two flights up from the restaurant.

As depressing as my room in the Van Cortlandt was, Eric's was ten times more depressing. There were three primary reasons.

1. It was a third the size of my uptown living quarters which now seemed spacious.

2. It had no windows . . .or should I say IT HAD NO WINDOW. Eric explained that decades ago a law was passed that apartments had to have at least one window. Landlords figured out the law didn't say it had to be a window to the outside, so they put a window in an interior wall. Eric's apartment had had an interior window until it was bricked up to make single-room rentals out of the apartments. Generations of building inspectors had been paid not to notice.
3. In the middle of this tiny room was a bathtub. Yes, right in the middle. Eric had used his newfound carpentry skills to build a box around the bathtub. And he built a cover for the box so that when he was not taking a bath. he could use it for food preparation or writing. Yes, Eric was writing. He was writing a novel. And here we came to the real reason he invited me and paid for dinner. I was an English major and he wanted me to fix it before he submitted it to publishers. Afraid that if I refused his mood would change and I'd end up in pieces in the tub in the windowless room, I hastily agreed. He would make me a copy he said and deliver it.

I asked what it was about.

"Turkey."

"Turkey? Like . . ."

"The country," he finished before I could say "like Thanksgiving dinner?"

"It's based on my six months in Turkey. It's like *On the Road*, only in Turkey."

"Great!"

I sort of stalled after saying "Great."

I bade Eric and his bathtub farewell and headed back uptown to the Van Cortlandt trying to remember everything I had ever learned about Turkey. I didn't get past the B's. The Bosporus and baklava.

I was pretty disoriented when I got off the IRT. I missed my stop if getting off before your stop can be called missing it. I got off at 110th Street instead of 114th. I preferred 110th Street's original name, Cathedral Parkway, because it drew attention to St. John the Divine, a few blocks away.

I liked having a Cathedral within spitting distance of where I lived. It was just a block away from my trusty Amsterdam Avenue phone booth. When I made a call, I turned around to look at its towering spires while I talked. Or, I should say, its truncated towering spires. I loved that it was perpetually unfinished so much so that everyone called it St. John the Unfinished. Sometimes I went to mass there even though it was Episcopal just so I could look at the statues of Joan of Arc, William Shakespeare and Abraham Lincoln that popped out from various niches and chapels. It was so dark and medieval inside. I knew it was supposed to be the Episcopalian answer to St. Patrick's but I cared for it so much more. It was haunted, mysterious and almost always empty. Good for reinforcing my undergraduate depressions.

So instead of walking up Broadway, I cut across 110th to Amsterdam to pay my respects and once again think about how poorly lit and gloomy-looking this weird, oversized misfit of an Upper West Side building was. Where's Quasimodo when you need him?

I turned down 113th and about halfway to Broadway a short, shabbily dressed man in his thirties approached me. The transaction was pretty straightforward.

"Give me your money," he said.

He had his hand in his jacket pocket. It could be a knife. It could be a gun. It could be a hand.

"OK," I said, too surprised to be scared. "I don't have much though."

I reached in my pocket and produced my wallet.

"Give it to me," he said.

It was the days before I had my life in my wallet. No credit cards. No irreplaceable photos of beloveds. Not even a driver's license since that was back at my parents.

"There's only three dollars in here," he whined

"I know. I'm a student."

"Jesus Christ. How can you walk around with only three dollars? How can you live?"

I stiffened. My pride was injured. In an offended voice I repeated, "I'm a student. Students generally don't have money."

"Here. Let me show you how to make a quick buck." At this point, he removed his hand from his pocket. He had been holding a wire, a wire sort of like a coat hanger wire only thinner. It was looped at one end. He walked over to the Buick in front of us and pushed the loop through the rubber gasket at the top of the window and then expertly slipped it over the car door button.

An "in those days aside" in those days, there were no car alarms; there were no keyless entries; and there were no wireless key fobs. There was only a button that looked like a golf tee that went up and down when you put a key in the lock on the door handle.

The car door button popped up; my new friend in criminal enterprise opened the door. Then he tried the glove compartment. It was locked. He reached in his other pocket and took out a miniature crowbar. All the finesse he exhibited opening the car was now gone. He smashed the crowbar against the glove compartment until it yielded, looked around to see if there were any witnesses and pulled out the glove compartment contents. After winnowing through papers, he found five ten-dollar bills and a man's signet ring.

"Here's twenty," he said, handing me two of the tens. "I'll keep the ring. Might be worth something."

He closed the car door, turned away from me and started walking down the street.

After a few steps, he turned and waved. "Make yourself some money."

He pointed to the twisted wire.

"You can make one of these yourself."

My first felony, I thought.

I tucked the two tens in my pocket and walked home with a bounce in my step.

Chapter Thirteen

In late spring I ran I into Grant, who told me there was a special pledge class at the fraternity in a week and my name was on the list. I wouldn't be able to abandon the Van Cortlandt, but I would be able to plan my sprint to freedom.

And so a week later, wearing a white shirt and tie, I showed up at Phi Epsilon Pi, housed in a decrepit brownstone on the south side of 113th Street a hundred feet from my old dorm, Carman Hall and a hundred feet from the Van Cortlandt, whose trash-littered back yard abutted the fraternity's trash-littered backyard.

Years later I discovered that Phi Ep, as we shortened it, was founded in the late 19th century as a Jewish fraternity. Jews, Blacks and Roman Catholics who managed to get into college had trouble being admitted to traditional fraternities which often had charters with restrictive language. So these groups founded their own. After World War II, most restrictive covenants were abandoned by university mandates. This put economic pressure on these special needs frats to open up as well. In the transition, fraternities like Phi Ep hedged their bets by restricting admission to "men of good character." By 1969, the fraternity system was falling apart, as were universities. "Good character" was shortened to mean "character." On that ground, I qualified.

Grant and Wu had sponsored me so I was assured of a place, but I still had to go through an official induction ceremony. There were six of us: Farrell, a young man from Montana who was like a template for Sam Shepard and who wore some kind of hybrid rancher/bomber jacket; Mike, a student of Greek descent at the Mining School; Ray, the Engineering School undergraduate who I had spent Christmas with; Mitch, a Buffalo pledge who was the Jewish placeholder; Randall a generic pre-med who entertained people by reciting the names of the 206 bones in an adult human body in alphabetical order, and me.

Our pledge ceremony took place in the first-floor recreation room. It was poorly lit and decorated with old moldy sofas that were pushed up against windows that had ornate early 20th-century iron gates covering them. The whole room was paneled with a veneer you would use to decorate a VFW in Appalachia.

Apparently, Phi Ep had never pledged an interior designer or the scion of a furniture manufacturer.

There were about fifteen fraternity brothers present. The great unmentionable which Grant had mentioned was that nine of the brothers were graduating Seniors, thereby creating a financial crisis and also thereby assuring my admission.

I knew little about fraternities, but I did know enough to be worried about debauchery and humiliation. So when we six pledges were lined up in the front hall and given lit candles to walk into the ceremony with, I was concerned this was the beginning of some ceremony in which the candle would end up up my bum.

We were told this was a solemn ceremony and walked solemnly in and stood in front of three solemn judges, the executive tribunal of Phi Ep.

We were asked our names and our reasons for pledging. I said a desire for brotherhood in an otherwise anonymous city. I did not mention a desire to escape Dorothy Dutto.

The ceremony began with a long lecture on Greek societies by the fraternity scribe. And then the fraternity president gave another long lecture on the meaning of men of good character. And then the fraternity vice president gave another long lecture on the responsibilities of brothers toward one another.

Randall was called forward and asked to be the pledges' agent. He was told to raise his right hand and recite.

The pledge began:

> *I believe in Phi Epsilon Pi and its guiding principles. We believe in promoting in our fraternity and in our lives justice that reflects the universal values of our brotherhood. We will aid each other not only during our educational sojourn but throughout our*

lives . We will come to the aid of any Phi Epsilon Pi brother at any time, any place and any circumstance.

We will dedicate our lives to the highest ideals and we will walk proudly among our fellow man as men of good character, ready to extend a helping hand to anyone in need.

Through friendship, we seek truth and honor.

I offer my fellow pledges as seekers of tolerance through our service to our fellow man and to God.

Randall was thanked and retreated back to our line of pledges. I thought this a most unexpectedly civilized ceremony and began to relax. It didn't seem like the candle would end up my bum.

The President then said "And now I move that we accept these pledges as the newest members of the Beta Chapter of Phi Epsilon Pi at Columbia University."

Before he could say "All in Favor," there was a voice in the back of the room.

"I thought we agreed that we weren't going to use the word God anymore." The speaker was like a which-one-does-not-belong cartoon. We all were sort of preppy. He looked like an electrocuted version of Frank Zappa.

"Now, Rufus. That's not so. I said we would consider your request. And we did. And since you are the only atheist in the fraternity, the rest of us decided that we will stand by our various religious beliefs and our traditional oath. God stays in the oath."

"Fuck you," was Rufus's measured reply.

"What?"

"You heard me. Fuck you. And Fuck your God."

There was an uncomfortable shifting.

"Now, Rufus, there's no need to get blasphemous."

"The fuck there isn't. This is a fraternity not a cult. We're fraternity brothers not the Brothers of St. Francis."

There was more uncomfortable shifting and another voice said "Calm down."

"I know my rights in this fraternity," Rufus continued. "We vote pledges in unanimously. I'm voting No. No pledges. No class."

The President now started to look uncomfortable. "Umm, Rufus. You know why we're having this Spring class. We have to have members ready to take up residence in September."

"Because we need money to keep going. Well, maybe we should just fold." He added with a sneer "Maybe it's God's will."

At this point the room, which had been merely shifting from one foot to the other, burst into chaos.

"Rufus is a doofus," someone pronounced.

"You hippie scum," one rather large frat brother screamed. And then he jumped on Rufus. Two more brothers jumped on the attacker and tried to pull him off the infidel. A few others got in a heated argument and began throwing punches at each other. Soon the whole room was hollering and knocking over lamps and pummeling each other on the sad furniture.

Randall, the pledge who had given the oath screamed at the top of his lungs. "Stop Stop Stop." I think the sight of so many potential bones arranged unalphabetically moved him to action.

Miraculously, everyone did stop.

"Look. It's not worth it. I have a solution. I'm the one who gave the pledge. I'm the one who said God. I will withdraw from pledging. Someone else can give the oath without God in it. And then you can save the fraternity."

Randall began to cry. It was clear that of all us who were new pledges, he was the one who really wanted to be in this fraternity. The rest of us just wanted a cheap place to sleep.

Randall hung his head, his candle still burning.

Here and there throughout the room, the brothers began to chuckle. They disengaged from their physical and verbal battles, restored furniture to an upright position and picked up the dingy lamps from the corners where they had been flung.

It was eerie, almost as if a supernatural force had restored order. Rufus stood up smiling, seeming none the worse for his attacker's assault.

Rufus came up to the front of the room where we pledges were standing.

He said, "By the powers vested in me by the Beta Chapter of Phi Epsilon Pi fraternity under a charter granted by Columbia University formerly known as King's College, I welcome you as new Brothers of our fraternal order."

The room erupted into cheers and someone rolled in a keg. Someone else brought in a large cake.

This had all been a hoax.

The President, whose name was Jordan, explained that the hazing consisted of staging a mock controversy that varied from year to year. The brothers would then appear to dissolve into a frenzy of argument, recriminations and assaults until one of the pledges begged this very unfraternal behavior stop. At that point, the Brothers would be satisfied there had been sufficient bonding to assure that the new pledges would care enough about the fraternity and its members to be more than just young men sleeping under the same roof. And this is the way it had been since 1904.

Randy was carried around the room on a bunch of shoulders. He knocked out a few ceiling tiles during the celebration.

And so that was that. I wasn't forced to have sex with a prostitute; I didn't have to take my clothes off and run naked through a line of paddles and I didn't have to drink to unconsciousness. In fact, no one had more than a couple of beers. The cake was more popular than the keg.

Grant and Wu walked up to me smiling. "Congratulations, bro," Wu said with his Hawaiian inflection. Grant said "Wasn't that great! Last year it was about parliamentary procedure. Personally, I like the God controversy better."

I walked back to the Van Cortlandt thinking "Finally someplace I belong."

Chapter Fourteen

I had never really worked. I mean, I worked very hard at my studies in high school, but I never held a job, other than the one day I spent unloading watermelons at the grocery store, a job that almost led to my demise when I quit and told my father who promptly tried to strangle me. That was the first time I realized the price he paid for fighting his way off the farm, out of the steel mills and into the middle class. And here I was at nineteen, never paid for a day's labor.

My parents earned just enough money so I couldn't receive a scholarship. I knew that the tuition, as modest as it seems now, combined with the extraordinary amount of spending money they gave me to make me appear to be gentry, put a strain on their finances. I called them to tell them I was not returning for the summer. Instead, I was going to get a job in the City after classes ended and that I would not accept money from them after I got a job. Once again, they were patiently resigned to my twists and turns, but I thought appreciative.

I made a half-hearted attempt to find work at school, but when I went to student employment, I was yelled at for trying to take work from a scholarship student. Rejected by academia, I decided I wanted a job, but I wanted a job that was suitable. I was a job snob.

The Columbia student newspaper, *The Spectato*r, had a help wanted column. This would be a good place to begin. One ad appealed to me: "Blind woman needs reader for research. Will pay." Perfect. Charitable and Academic at the same time. A phone number accompanied the brief ad.

I called the number from the Amsterdam Avenue phone booth. A woman answered. I was responding to the help wanted ad in the Columbia newspaper I said and was told to wait a minute until Mrs. Harris could come to the phone. When Mrs. Harris spoke it was with clipped tones. "Well, what is it?" I explained that I was calling at her ad's behest.

"I hope you like Thucydides. You do know who Thucydides is, don't you?"

"Yes, ma'am. Athenian historian and general. *The Peloponnesian Wars.*"

"Well, you're not a fool, young man. I hope you're not a radical."

"No ma'am. Just a student." My heart sank. I had debased myself. For a job. That I didn't even have yet.

"Be here Tuesday at one o'clock sharp." She repeated, "Sharp."

She gave me the address in the East Seventies and then hung up.

I woke up Tuesday morning full of anxiety. I got dressed and selected my one tie, the one I had worn to Mrs. Moore's dinner. At 11:30 a.m., I got on the subway after buying that day's *Times* at the news kiosk. I thought it would give me an extra look of being informed.

I had planned my route meticulously and knew I'd arrive with a half-hour to spare.

But I didn't anticipate the vagaries of public transportation. Halfway down to 59th Street, the IRT stopped between stations. The lights went off in the car. The doors were shut. The fans stopped blowing overhead. I heard a ripple of "What the fucks?" among the more experienced passengers. We sat. Ten minutes. Twenty minutes. Thirty minutes. Forty-five minutes. Fifty minutes. Finally, we inched our way to Eight-Sixth Street. I jumped out and started to run to the east, across Amsterdam, across Central Park West, across Central Park. I heard Mrs. Harris say "Sharp." I knew she meant "Sharp."

Finally, at about one o'clock, still ten minutes from my destination, I ran into a phone booth. The phone was out of order. I started to run again. By now I was sweating in the cool May afternoon. People were beginning to look at me. People didn't behave like this on the East Side. I finally reached the apartment building at about 1:15. I introduced myself to the doorman who rang Mrs. Harris.

"Your one o'clock is here, Mrs. Harris," he said.

"He's late. Tell him I won't see him," she squawked through the intercom.

"Please, I'm sorry. The subway . . . ." I yelled hoping that the intercom would pick up my pleas. I heard a click of a receiver being replaced.

"She's like that, son," the doorman said. "Sorry. You must be coming from the Westside. Some idiot walked off a train and got himself electrocuted on the third rail."

I turned around so the doorman would not see me cry. I left the building, shoulders hunched. I was also famished from terror and exertion. I walked by a coffee shop and stepped inside. It was much more expensive than my West Side food suppliers, but I sat at the counter anyway and ordered a hamburger.

The waitress asked me if something was wrong and said she wouldn't charge me for the Coke. I buried my sadness in *The Times* I was still carrying. The lead story on the front page was by a reporter improbably yet charmingly named Sylvan Fox who had written an article about Black (which were still called Negroes in *The Times'* headline) and Puerto Rican students ending their two-week blockade of the City College of New York South campus.

I cheered up. I had an idea.

After the hamburger, I looked around for a phone booth. There was one by the coat rack up front. I paid, took a dime of my change and called Mrs. Harris.

The same female intermediary answered the phone. I lowered my voice.

"Hello," I confidently greeted her, "This is Sylvan Fox, reporter for *The New York Times*. We're thinking of doing a human interest story on Mrs. Harris. Is she in?"

The intermediary made some flustered noises and then said in an across-the-room voice, "Ethel, it's *The New York Times*. They want to do a story on you."

There was an excited shuffle and after twenty seconds or so, Mrs. Harris answered the phone with a formal, dignified, extended "Yes?"

"Hi, Mrs. Harris," I began. "This isn't *The New York Times*. This is the student you were supposed to meet with today. There was a body on the subway tracks and that was why I was late. Please give me another chance."

Silence. More silence. Still more silence. Then a sputter. "I know President Cordier. I'll have you expelled." And with that, she hung up the phone.

For a moment, all I had worked for passed before me. Nineteen and finished. I would return to Rochester in disgrace. I would never get another college placement. I would work the counter at a hardware store.

But then I perked up. I realized that not once had I actually stated my name to Mrs. Harris. I reviewed all communication and understood that she had so little interest in who I was that she never asked. And I had called her only from public pay phones.

I had gotten a reprieve from the hardware store.

I was on the East Side already so I decided to celebrate my good fortune by taking the Second Avenue bus down to the Strand Bookstore on lower Broadway. An afternoon among used books would banish Mrs. Harris from my mind. Maybe I'd even find a new translation of Thucydides I could send to her anonymously.

Chapter Fifteen

The Strand Bookstore was much smaller then. I recently read it has over 200 employees. In the Sixties, it was well-known among cognoscenti, but not famous and celebrated and not a place where 200 people could even comfortably fit. There were other, smaller bookstores on the side streets of lower Broadway then. But most were just small dusty single proprietor mountains of uncategorized paper. The Strand was the emporium version of these stores, not as dusty, but still not clean better lit, but still piled to the rafters with thousands of miscellaneous volumes. And busy. Clerks hustling on the floor customers buying and selling books, and booklovers making arcane demands.

I loved it.

I spent about a half-hour just browsing randomly when employment lightning struck. The Sheridan Square Bookstore had rejected me. I would try the Strand.

I walked up to the most proprietary looking person in the place and asked him for a job.

I had asked Fred Bass, whose obituary I read in *The Times* forty-nine years later. Of course, neither he nor I knew he would become the famous Fred Bass with a *Times*' obituary. Fred functioned as a sort of general manager in short shirt-sleeves while his father, Ben, the founder, sat in the corner in an old shiny black suit like some Torah scholar divining which books would bring how much.

Old man Bass had started in the book business on Fourth Avenue just before the Depression. There were forty-eight bookstores on Fourth then, and after the Crash there were a lot less. Bass somehow survived and when his son Fred took over in the mid-Fifties, he moved the store to a building at Broadway and Twelfth. And this is where I found myself late on a Tuesday afternoon in May, with dry mouth and the sweats, asking Fred for a job.

"You in college?" Fred asked.

"Yes, sir."

"Where?"

"Columbia."

"What are you studying?"

"English."

"Who wrote *Pamela*?"

"*Or Virtue Rewarded*?" I added the subtitle.

"Yes."

"Samuel Richardson, sir."

"Joe," he shouted to someone who looked like a cross between Jackie Gleason and Phil Silver. "Get this guy started in the basement tomorrow."

And the Gates of Heaven opened.

I don't know how many employees existed in cubbyholes and annexes of the rented building, but the ones I remember are Fred and his father, who certainly acted as if they never read a book for pleasure; the manager Burt Britton, who became enough of a famous Strand character to end up with his own obituary in *The Times*; the assistant manager, James, a writer who looked like Robert Redford after a couple rounds in Harry Hope's saloon and who had a much more lucrative side gig writing porn; Joe, who certainly never read a book, had the personality and intelligence and good looks of Curly of The Three Stooges and whose sole purpose seemed to be to panic; and Edward, who had an expense account and zoomed around Manhattan in an ancient red Carmen Ghia, taking authors, reviewers and agents to lunch so he could buy their review copies for pennies on the dollar. There were various book slaves who dragged cartons of the same title and occasionally disappeared into the upper floors of the building where the books by the foot were kept. This was a lucrative cynical ancillary business pitched to decorators and set designers. Need 100 feet of books with pink covers for a set in the next Doris Day movie? The book slaves would make sure they matched, even if the subject matters didn't. The upper floors were also occupied by the John Jay College of Criminal Justice. It was easy to tell the long-haired slaves from the law enforcement officers of tomorrow. One never met a text he liked; the other never met a text he didn't.

When I arrived at the store, the "new" location close to Union Square was about 10 years old. There were no tote bags, T-shirts, bright murals, author signings, recommended lists. It was just a big old used bookstore which largely thrived on review copies—free books given to reviewers by publishers. This is how books took off. Free samples. And reviewers supplemented their thin incomes by selling these review copies—mostly to The Strand. The lowest prices went for fiction titles. The classic Strand advertised over **8 Miles of Books**. Four miles of them were fiction that would never sell. And the basement where I took up residence was the graveyard of those four miles. It was my job to figure out how to stack 20 copies of Larry Woiwode's latest *What I'm Going to Do I Think* or the 30 copies of Donald Barthelmé's *Snow White* or 40 copies of John Barth's *Lost in the Funhouse*. This was, of course, impossible, so I spent most of the day hiding out and reading some of the eight miles of books. There were four of us in the basement: Mona, the billing clerk, and the only woman who worked at the store; Robert, who was looking for his place in Village culture; and, eventually, Tommy, who had bolted from military school in Virginia and who looked like a teenage member of Jefferson Airplane.

I soon developed a loner routine. I would retreat at six every day to my welfare hotel where my true north community hung out. I ate lunch alone in the same lunch place in Union Square and always ordered the dollar sixty-nine special which would fill me up with a soda, a variation on meatloaf, mashed potatoes, a droopy, canned vegetable and fruit in some stage of sugar shock. I only stayed Downtown once or twice to go to a movie. There was no Tower Records, or clever restaurants or hip bars. There were no sock shops or even fortunetellers in storefronts. This was the septic foot of Manhattan . . . squatters, drug addicts, homeless sleeping on cardboard, squeegee men, drifters, grifters, muggers looking for fresh uptown victims, and boys and girls who sold street corner sex. This corner of Manhattan was aflame, but not with the naughty abandon of Sodom or Gomorrah, but with Despair and Desperation from the Slough of Despond. These were the New Yorkers who were the untouchables, trying to stay alive. This was New York's New Delhi.

But back to Robert, Mona, and Tommy.

Robert was probably year or two older than I was. He was enormously serious and enormously sad. He was in charge of "I through P." He always came to work in a pressed shirt; his moustache freshly groomed, his fuzzy hair tightly cropped. One afternoon near the end of a day loitering in the stacks, he asked me if I wanted to go to a movie. I was sort of thrilled to be asked to do something Downtown. "Sure," I asked. "What?" "It" called *Titicut Follies* and it" really controversial." I had never heard of it but, hey, it was worth the investment for a friendship. To say *Titicut Follies* was controversial was like saying The Carolina Reaper was a pretty hot pepper. The documentary, by Frederick Wiseman was a stark record of the lives of the inmates of an old-fashioned but still very much functioning, mental hospital in Massachusetts. *Titicut Follies* referred to the show the confined put on once a year. The word Titicut was the native American name for the idyllic river that ran by the grounds. The river was the only peaceful part about the mental hospital. Abuse, neglect, forced feedings, mandatory stripping, humiliation on top of horrifying scenes of the torment of mental illness had kept this out of theaters for two years. It was the only movie ever banned in America for reasons other than obscenity or revealing national secrets. For a while on its contested journey, only psychiatrists were allowed to see it. Every once in a while, it would surface and like whale spotting, mental health porn enthusiasts would rush to see it. But I knew nothing of this. I was just along for the ride.

After 84 minutes of witnessing the seventh circle of hell, rings one through three, Robert asked me if I wanted to go to dinner. The scenes of forced feedings made me wonder if I could keep anything down. I declined and rode the rails Uptown to my safe madhouse.

Robert and I never really connected again. Once on my way to my alphabetical entombment, I went down one of his aisles. I surprised him and before he could close the book he was reading, I saw its title. In academic embossing it read *Homosexuality*. I said reflexively, "It's OK." Three weeks later he was gone.

You have to realize the Stonewall Riots had just taken place on June 29th and the Stonewall was a six-minute walk from the Strand. I can't recall anyone either at the Strand or

Uptown mentioning the riots. Gay men and lesbians still lived in shadows, fearing persecution, attacks, employment discrimination and arrest. Despite the civil rights' movement, the Black Power, the rise of feminism and student activism, Gay was not beautiful; it was the last taboo. Evie might have slept in the same bed with a Black man, but she would never have slept in the same bed as a lesbian.

Mona did the billing and sat at the foot of the basement stairs. Mona was strangely beautiful—like a gaunt, unaffected, very tall Lily Tomlin. She dressed in bright muumuus because although she was very thin, she was also very pregnant. With no husband or boyfriend in sight. Unmarried pregnant women were usually ostracized and put somewhere out of sight then. Mona was very much visible and occupied a warm-blooded place in the cold-blooded staff's hearts. We brought her small gifts, parts of our lunches like the soup or salad, candies and once I brought her flowers. I loved her, but since she was a full decade older than I was, there was little doubt but that I would not raise her child.

Mona typed up invoices all day long on an old manual typewriter. She used carbon paper, of course, and was always throwing a "damn" or a "shit" at the carbons. She billed the institutions, the high rollers, the decorators, the collectors and took the phone calls when there was a billing error, or, more likely when someone needed to reopen an unpaid account.

One Saturday, I came in to work and she and I were the only people in the basement. Most of the upstairs staff didn't show up either. Fred was furious. I asked Mona where everyone was. She looked at me, weary from her heavy maternal burden, sighed and said, "They went to some music concert Upstate on a farm. Fred is furious." I was promoted, that Saturday only, to the sales floor.

Mona worked under her own music cascading from an old brown Philco radio. One day while John Lennon's *Give Peace a Chance* was playing, she asked me why anyone would listen to a song with lyrics like "All New York City is hippies and tramps." I processed for a moment and said, "Mona, he's singing 'All we are saying is give peace a chance.'" "Oh," she said unfazed. " I didn't think it sounded right."

Chapter Sixteen

In late July a new hire appeared to take over Robert's "I through P." Tommy was lanky, sort of rock-and-roll with long blond clean hair. He told everyone often about his escape from military school. I was intrigued. I had never known anyone in a military school. He was very well-read and was annoyed that he was stuck in fiction. He wanted to maintain the poetry section. Burt, the manager, laughed at him and said go to Steloff's place. There's no money in poetry. Burt was referring, of course, to Frances Steloff's Gotham Book Mart in the Diamond District where you could take your self-published chapbook and just put it anywhere in the store. Tommy retorted, "All the rest is mere fine writing," which he told me was a quote from his favorite poet Paul Verlaine.

One day around noon, Tommy came over to "P-Z" and said, "Hey, wanna go to my place for lunch." Still eager for a Strand friend, I easily agreed. His apartment was in a squatter's building about three blocks away. We had to climb up to the fourth floor because the elevator was broken. There were open bags of trash on the stairs. The whole building seemed unoccupied, even for a squatter's building. He opened the door to his apartment and there were more open bags of trash inside. There was only natural light and precious little of that. The refrigerator had some small amount of take-out which he offered me, and one bottle of beer which he also offered me. "Aren't you having anything?" I asked. "No, I'm not hungry." Then he added "At all."

I ate the take-out, wondering if I would die, found a church key to open the beer and took a preliminary sip.

"I actually asked you over because I need to get rid of this refrigerator."

"Oh," I said, suddenly feeling more like the help than a potential friend. He unplugged it and started pulling the filthy though oxymoronically empty refrigerator toward the window or toward the opening where there was once a window.

"Have you ever seen a refrigerator fly?" Tommy asked. And with that riddle, we pushed the refrigerator through the windowless window where it flew clumsily four stories down the airshaft of the empty building.

I looked down and saw a mass of tangled televisions and refrigerators punctuated by a wringer washer or two. Were they all his?

"Let's get back. We're gonna be late," he concluded.

And we were. Burt sneered "Shooting up, boys?" He should only know.

Years later I saw a young man on television. It was Tommy. And although his first name was Tom, his last name was now revealed to be Verlaine. He became the poet he read. He was as famous as Verlaine the First. He dated Patti Smith. He escaped that military academy with his best friend Richard Hell. And they formed the most intellectual of punk rock bands, Television.

I thought of the appliances at the bottom of the airshaft and reflected on how close the most influential band of the Seventies came to being called Refrigerator.

I was getting restless. I longed for light. I was tired of reading poorly bound books. I wanted to live upstairs. I wanted to breathe among art, philosophy, history, economics. I wanted facts, not fiction. One day on my break, I was looking at a book of Breugel paintings.

"You like Breugel? You know he never painted portraits."

I looked up. It was Pasqual. I never had much to do with Pasqual. He was the Enforcer, or at least that's how Burt used him. He sat on a stool most Saturdays looking out for shoplifters or he checked bags or he lifted heavy boxes. Pasqual was Mexican-American but was born and raised in Brooklyn. He looked like Pancho Villa but he sounded like Howard Cosell. It turned out that Pasqual was an artist, in fact, a painter and studied at the Art Students League like Evie's neighbor whenever he could afford it. I spent more and more of my breaks upstairs as he annotated the art books. He had a penchant for unknown artists . . . minor Impressionists, schools of anonymous assistants, the Dutch artist collectives. He knew the art history texts backwards but he lived for the footnotes.

☮ ☮ ☮

In late August, my friend Bill asked me if I wanted to drive his brother-in-law's BMW 1800 across country to Phoenix. Bill had to pick it up in a New York City showroom. His brother-in-law was heir to the Spiegel catalog fortune which sounds like a joke until you realize that department store catalogs like Spiegel and Sears were the Amazon of their day and that Spiegel, in particular, offered no-interest credit. The company's motto was "We Trust the People" and apparently the brother-in-law trusted Bill.

Everyone read *On The Road* then. And a 1969 BMW 1800 sedan sure bested Dean Moriarty's 1949 Hudson. I was the antithesis of Sal Paradise; Bill was the polar opposite of Dean. And Phoenix was somewhere near Sal and Dean's mythical Mexico. I called my parents. My mother cried once again and said she'd give Bill some cookies to bring down with him. I was a little embarrassed. I didn't think Sal and Dean ate cookies. Just plugs of tobacco.

I went to work and told Pasqual. As I was telling him, I thought, Pasqual would be great on a cross country trip. He would be a great Dean. So it would be more like Sal and Sal and Dean. "Why don't you come with us?" "Deal." Pasqual was in.

We gave our notice to Burt separately but on the same day. Burt, who was similar in temperament to Colonel

Kurtz in *Apocalypse Now,* only with books instead of helicopters, cared little about me. But when Pasqual, who had been there for two years, gave notice, all hell broke loose. Burt, who had a permanently unlit cigar affixed to his lip, spit out tobacco-soaked words charging betrayal and perfidy. The one true artist the Strand could lay claim to was leaving home.

I visited my parents for a few days and then came down on the train with Bill. We went to the BMW showroom and drove the shiny brown car right off the showroom floor on 57th Street traffic. We drove to Brooklyn and picked up Pasqual who was in travel mode with a red bandana, a duffel bag and a guitar.

It only remained to leave the Van Cortlandt. I waited until La Dutto left for the day and then Bill, Pasqual and I packed the BMW with my modest collection of books, clothes and household goods. I had gotten permission from Phi Ep to store my belongings in an unoccupied room that no one ever wanted to live in on the first floor behind the recreation room pledge site.

I had paid my own rent since June. Mrs. Dutto reluctantly accepted it by the week to help me out financially. I left my last week's rent in an envelope and shoved it through the grille at her concierge station. Two twenties and two quarters. I knocked on doors and said goodbye to Andy, Tom, Pat, Carmen, Dan and anyone I met on the stairs. Plato's cave. That was it. Plato's cave. Soon I would not be seeing a shadow world but a real one. Or was this the real one? Thrilled, yet terrified; expectant, yet full of dread. The

Van Cortlandt had been my home. I had come in defeat and left in triumph. Or at least in one piece. It was my first year as an adult. It was my first year of compassion. It was my first year of wisdom. It was my first year of life.

Bill drove the BMW to the West Side Highway. Soon we were crossing the George Washington Bridge. Out of the City.

Hosey v. Club Van Cortlandt, 299 F. Supp. 501 (S.D.N.Y. 1969)

U.S. District Court for the Southern District of New York - 299 F. Supp. 501 (S.D.N.Y. 1969)
March 24, 1969

---

299 F. Supp. 501 (1969)
Andrew HOSEY, Plaintiff,
v.
CLUB VAN CORTLANDT and John J. Hallohan, Defendants.
No. 68-Civ. 4498.

United States District Court S. D. New York.
March 24, 1969.

***502** Harold J. Rothwax, New York City, Director, Mobilization for Youth Legal Services Unit, for plaintiff; by Lester Evens, Jonathan Weiss, and Michael B. Rosen, New York City, of counsel.

Nathaniel Borah, New York City, for defendants; by Lawrence S. Borah, New York City, of counsel.

CROAKE, District Judge.

MEMORANDUM

Andrew Hosey, a tenant in a residential hotel, brings this action to enjoin the hotel and its manager from instituting a summary proceeding to evict him. He has placed two interesting questions before this court on a motion for a preliminary injunction. May a state court constitutionally evict a hold-over tenant when the landlord seeks the eviction in retaliation for the tenant's attempts to organize his co-tenants to complain to public officials about health and building code violations in the building? If the first question is answered in the negative, should this court enjoin this landlord from bringing a summary proceeding to evict? We answer both questions in the negative and deny the motion for a preliminary injunction.

The complaint, filed November 14, 1968, alleges that Andrew Hosey has been a week-to-week tenant in the Club Van Cortlandt for over two years. During his stay he has encouraged other tenants to try to get the landlord to make repairs necessary for their health and safety, and has filed complaints with city officials. On August 21, 1968, after a notice was circulated to the tenants, a meeting was held in plaintiff's room to discuss conditions in the building and to consider making complaints to appropriate officials. The following day plaintiff was informed by a hotel employee that his rent would be raised. On August 27, 1968 he received a letter from the hotel manager that his room had been reserved for someone else as of September 3. Plaintiff sought to have the New York Supreme Court enjoin any eviction; his motion for a temporary injunction was denied on October 18, 1968. Plaintiff did not move out and ***503** on October 25 he received a formal notice to vacate the room by November 4 or the landlord would institute a summary proceeding to dispossess him. Plaintiff contends that the landlord wants to evict him in retaliation for the exercise of the rights of speech and assembly and the right to petition to redress grievances.

The defendants, the landlord and the hotel manager, deny all the critical allegations of the complaint except the state court decision and the seven-day notice to vacate. The manager has submitted an affidavit saying the landlord intends to institute a summary proceeding to recover possession.[1] The reason given for seeking eviction is:

"[T]hat Mr. Hosey has been quite late with his rent payments and the landlord has had to write letters and make calls in order to collect the money due him. The landlord has had much trouble in collecting his rent on time."[2]

I

Subject matter jurisdiction over this action derives from 28 U.S.C. § 1343. Injunctive relief is authorized by 42 U.S.C. § 1983 which provides:

"Every person who, under color of any statute, ordinance, regulation, custom, or usage, of any State or Territory, subjects, or causes to be subjected, any citizen of the United States or other person within the jurisdiction thereof to the deprivation of any rights, privileges, or immunities secured by the Constitution and laws, shall be liable to the party injured in an action at law, suit in equity, or other proper proceeding for redress."

The fact that the deprivation has not occurred, but is threatened, does not bar this court from providing relief.[3]

On a motion for a preliminary injunction, this court must weigh several factors to determine whether or not equity requires imposition of an injunction pending a full hearing and final determination of the action. Among these factors are the probability the movant will succeed on the merits, the harm that will befall the plaintiff if the motion is denied, and the harm that the defendant will suffer if it is granted.[4] On the merits, the question will be whether there is a threatened violation of a constitutional right for which there is no adequate remedy at law.[5]

II
CHANCE OF SUCCESS ON THE MERITS

We find that the plaintiff can prove the facts he has alleged. Copies of the several documents referred to in the complaint were attached to it. The defendants' contention that they seek an eviction because of tardiness in paying rent is unconvincing in light of the lack of specificity in the allegation of frequent late payments, the absence of threats to evict prior to the tenants' meeting, and the coincidence of the tenants' meeting and the landlord's threats to evict. We find in particular that the plaintiff will probably be able to prove that the overriding reason for the threats of eviction was retaliation against the plaintiff for his attempts to organize the tenants. The difficult question in determining the plaintiff's chance of success is the legal one: Is the plaintiff entitled to relief on the facts he has alleged?

***504** Plaintiff›s argument is along these lines: His attempts to organize the tenants to file complaints with city officials about conditions in the Club Van Cortlandt were protected by the first amendment.[6] Any state action penalizing him for the exercise of these rights would be a violation of the 14th amendment; an order of a state court evicting him, and enforcement thereof, would be «state action.» This court should enjoin a threatened violation of the 14th amendment under 42 U.S.C. § 1983. We will consider each step of this argument.

There can be no doubt of the right of a tenant to discuss the condition of his building with his co-tenants to encourage them to use legal means to remedy improper conditions, to hold meetings, and to inform public officials of the conditions. In short, a tenant can organize the other tenants of his building to improve living conditions. He has the protection afforded by the first amendment so long as he does not interfere with the rights of other guests or the property or contract rights of the landlord.[7] Since first amendment rights have been incorporated in the 14th amendment, the state can take no action to prevent or penalize their exercise.[8]

Prior Cases

It may be useful to refer to several decisions dealing with retaliatory evictions and injunctive relief.[9] ("Retaliation" will be used in the remainder of this memorandum to refer to any conduct intended to penalize a person for exercising a constitutional right.)

In Edwards v. Habib[10] the trial court did not permit a tenant to offer proof of a landlord›s retaliatory motive in a statutory eviction action. The Court of Appeals for the District of Columbia discussed the constitutional aspects of the case because of the rules of statutory construction[11] and reached the point in its analysis of weighing the interests of the landlord against those of the tenant.[12] It decided the case on the basis of statutory construction and public policy and ruled that proof of retaliation must be heard in District of Columbia eviction actions.

The constitutionality of a retaliatory eviction was first discussed in California in Abstract Investment Co. v. Hutchinson.[13] The court had before it an appeal from a judgment for a landlord in a detainer action raising the question of the constitutionality of retaliatory eviction. Relying on Shelley v. Kraemer[14] and subsequent cases, the court held that the 14th amendment required the trial court to receive evidence on the plaintiff›s motive for bringing the action. It noted further:

"* * * Certainly the interest in preserving the summary nature of an ***505** action cannot outweigh the interest of doing substantial justice. To hold the preservation of the summary proceeding of paramount importance would be analogous to the 'tail wagging the dog.'"[15]

The California Supreme Court ruled on the necessity of enjoining a retaliatory eviction in Hill v. Miller.[16] Plaintiff, a month-to-month tenant, had received a notice to vacate because of his race. He sought to enjoin the landlord from evicting him, but the court sustained a demurrer. In affirming, the California court said:

"* * * The Fourteenth Amendment does not impose upon the state the duty to take *positive* action to prohibit a private discrimination of the nature alleged here."[17]

It distinguished *Abstract Investment* as a case which held:

"* * * to make available to a discriminating landlord the aid and processes of a court in effecting a discrimination would involve the state in action prohibited by the Fourteenth Amendment."[18]

It thus appears that California requires evidence of retaliation to be heard in an eviction action, but will not enjoin the retaliatory institution of an eviction action.[19]

Tarver v. G. & C. Construction Co., a case decided in this court in 1964, is nearly identical with the present case.[20] The plaintiffs there complained to the health department about their clogged toilet. In the evening of the same day they received a notice of a 400 percent rent increase and a threat of eviction if they did not pay it. Judge MacMahon granted a preliminary injunction saying that «they will probably be able to prove upon trial that they are threatened with eviction solely because they exercised their constitutional right to petition for a redress of their grievances.»

It appears that the few courts which have touched on the issues of this case hold that retaliatory evictions violate the 14th amendment, but split on the question of whether they should be enjoined.

Constitutionality of Retaliatory Evictions

The right of a landlord to pick his tenants and to refuse to renew the tenancy of a person he finds undesirable for any reason is not in issue here. We are asked to determine the extent to which a landlord can use the judicial process in effecting a retaliatory eviction.

Section one of the 14th amendment prohibits the states from abridging privileges and immunities of citizens, taking life, liberty or property without due process, or denying equal protection of its laws to any person. There is no doubt today that judicial action in private disputes is a form of state action required for application of the amendment. In ***506** Shelley v. Kraemer[21] and Barrows v. Jackson,[22] the Supreme Court found that equal protection would be denied if a court enforced, or awarded damages for the breach of, an agreement under which property would not be sold to non-Caucasians. The application of a rule of law, such as the common law of libel applied by the lower courts in New York Times Co. v. Sullivan,[23] which penalizes a person for the exercise of a constitutional right is a violation of the 14th amendment and a court cannot award damages under it.

A retaliatory eviction would be judicial enforcement of private discrimination; it would require the application of a rule of law that would penalize a person for the exercise of his constitutional rights. A distinction can be drawn between a retaliatory eviction and the cases cited in that the constitutional infirmity inheres not in the agreement enforced nor in the rule of law being applied, but in the motive for which the landlord invokes state assistance. This distinction is not enough to render a retaliatory eviction constitutional.[24] Where, as in Griffin v. Maryland,[25] the state enforces trespass laws so as to enforce a private policy of discrimination, it denies equal protection.[26] In that situation, just as here, the reason state aid is invoked gives rise to the denial of equal protection.

The effect that a rule of law permitting retaliatory evictions would have on tenants cannot be discounted. There would be no point in a tenant trying to improve conditions in a building that he would not be allowed to continue to live in.[27] Permitting retaliatory evictions would thus inhibit him in the exercise of his constitutional rights[28] or, in the words of the Supreme Court, have a chilling effect.[29]

We accordingly hold that the 14th amendment prohibits a state court from evicting a tenant when the overriding reason the landlord is seeking the eviction is to retaliate against the tenant for an exercise of his constitutional rights.[30]

Injunctive Relief

The only legal mechanism for evicting a tenant in New York City is a special ***507** proceeding to recover real property,[31] usually referred to as a summary proceeding. In New York City the Civil Court has jurisdiction over such an action.

[32] A summary proceeding may be brought on five specified grounds, including holding over.[33] Although a tenant may plead any «legal or equitable defense» in his answer,[34] the plaintiff contends that the landlord-tenant part of the Civil Court will not permit the defense of retaliation to be raised.

The law is unsettled in New York whether retaliation is a defense to a holdover proceeding. A 1967 decision of the New York City Civil Court, in a summary proceeding brought by the New York City Housing Authority, holds that the ground upon which the Authority decided to terminate the tenancy was irrelevant.[35] More recently, the court held specifically that the defense of retaliation could not be raised.[36] On the other hand, the City Court of Birmingham permitted the defense to be raised in a summary proceeding.[37] In an action by this plaintiff to have the New York Supreme Court enjoin the currently threatened eviction, Justice Saul Streit denied a temporary injunction because «[in a summary proceeding] plaintiff can urge any lawful grounds to prevent his eviction.»[38]

If we were to find that New York had settled this question against raising the defense, we would be inclined to issue an injunction under 42 U.S.C. 1983.[39] Since it has not settled the question, the threat of a constitutional violation is not sufficiently strong to require us to interfere with the orderly progress of the case through the state courts.[40]

The plaintiff argues that even should the New York courts permit the defense to be raised, we should issue an injunction because of the chilling effect that the threat of litigation would have on tenant organizers. To accept his argument would be to substitute the federal courts for the state courts in all similar proceedings since the federal court would have to try the case to determine the landlord's motive. The situation here is thus different from the one in Dombrowski v. Pfister.[41]

We accordingly find that, although a retaliatory eviction would violate the 14th amendment, it is not clear that a violation is threatened in this case. We ***508** therefore find that the plaintiff will not succeed on the merits.[42]

III
HARM TO THE PARTIES PENDING FINAL DISPOSITION

Assuming that the plaintiff has been tardy in tendering his rent, the financial loss resulting from late payments on one room in a residential hotel would not be significant. Any "harm" coming to the landlord because of the plaintiff's exercise of his constitutional rights is not harm cognizable by this court. We accordingly find that the landlord would not be seriously harmed if the preliminary injunction were granted.

If the Landlord-Tenant Part of Civil Court does not allow the defense of retaliation to be raised in the summary proceeding that has been threatened, the plaintiff will have recourse to higher courts to see if either New York statutes or the Federal Constitution require that proof on the defense be heard. The judgment will automatically be stayed pending appeal.[43] Accordingly, the plaintiff will not be harmed if his motion for a preliminary injunction is denied.

IV
FINDINGS AND CONCLUSIONS

The following findings and conclusions flow from this discussion:

1. The plaintiff has a reasonably good chance of proving the facts alleged at trial.
2. An eviction ordered by a state court in an action begun to retaliate against a tenant for exercising his rights of speech and assembly to remedy building and health code violations in his building would be a violation of the 14th amendment.
3. Although the landlord in this case threatens to institute a summary proceeding to dispossess, there is no clear danger that a violation of the 14th amendment will occur since it is unsettled whether the New York courts will entertain a defense of retaliation for the exercise of constitutional rights.
4. Plaintiff therefore is not entitled to a permanent injunction as a matter of law.
5. Issuance or refusal to issue a preliminary injunction would cause no significant harm to the plaintiff or the defendants pending a final disposition of this action.
6. Accordingly, the motion for a preliminary injunction must be denied.

So ordered.

Made in the USA
Middletown, DE
18 April 2021

37724791R00080